DON Q

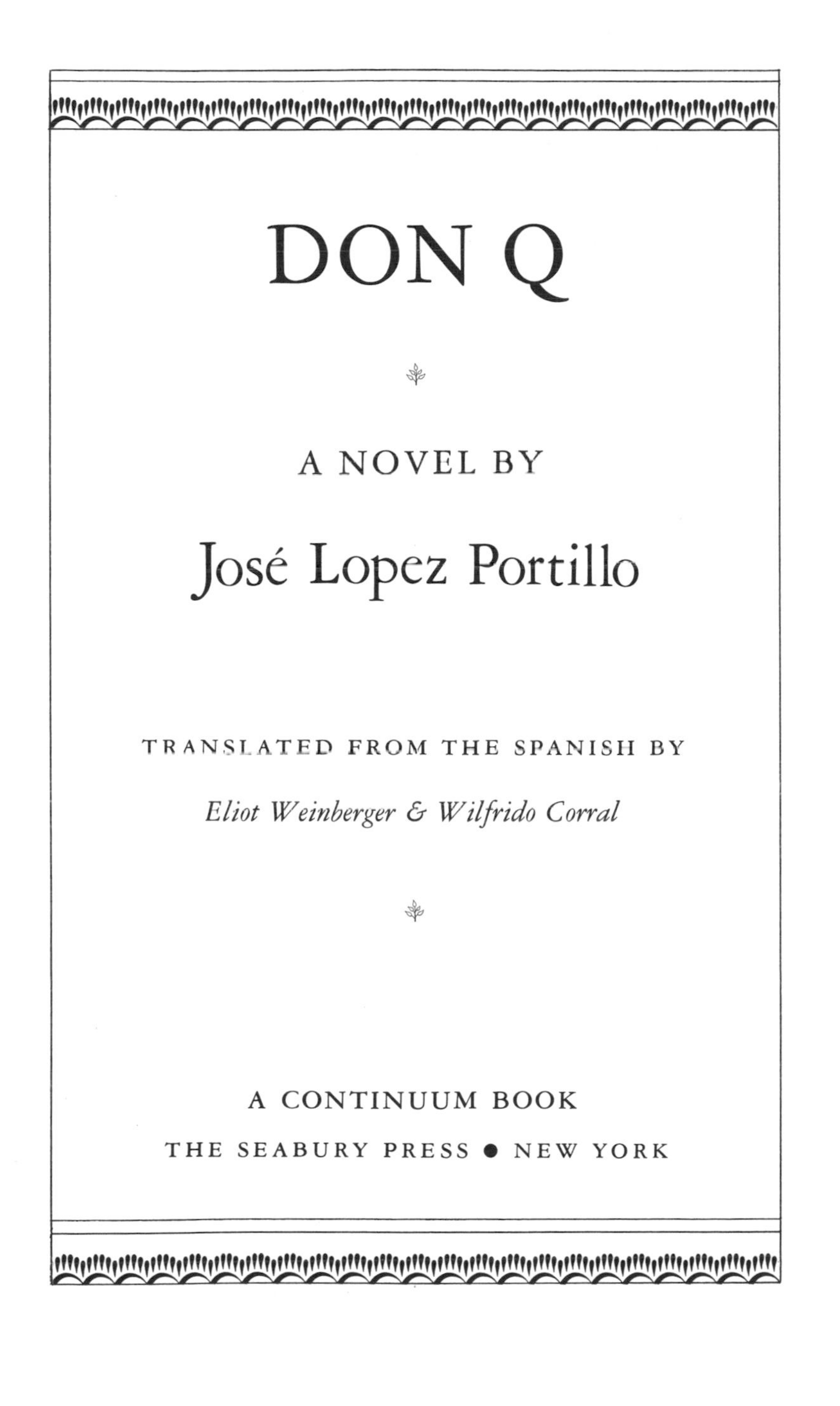

DON Q

A NOVEL BY

José Lopez Portillo

TRANSLATED FROM THE SPANISH BY

Eliot Weinberger & Wilfrido Corral

A CONTINUUM BOOK

THE SEABURY PRESS • NEW YORK

1976

The Seabury Press
815 Second Avenue
New York, New York 10017

Printed in the United States of America

Library of Congress Cataloging in Publication Data

Lopez-Portillo y Pacheco, José.
Don Q.
(A Continuum book)
I. Title.
Pz4.L864Do [PQ7298.22.06] 863 76-22613
ISBN 0-8164-9304-9

CONTENTS

CHAPTER I: *Which Examines the Law of the Universal Disproportion of Efficiency, the Inexhaustible Purse of Possibilities, Spiral Galaxies and Other Geometric Crudities.*

WHILE he pondered the Law of the Universal Disproportion of Efficiency with the ingenuity that characterized him, Don Q asked himself.

"Why doesn't air darken as one breathes?"

I suppose he asked himself this question feeling that he was consuming transparency with his respiration.

However, as he never worried about searching for the answers to certain questions he formulated, I believe this problem was not transcendent, nor have I ever worried about finding an occult sense to it, although I would have liked to enlighten him of the fact that one breathes a gas with a strong proportion of oxygen, but one does not breathe light. Nonetheless, I believe that, deep within, Don Q was a bit of a poet, and I'm afraid that he would have argued that, on occasion, there indeed are men who breathe light. It is not impossible that he believed something similar about himself.

He was convinced of the existence of a universal principle that he sometimes called "absolute squander," although on other occasions, with somewhat more petulance, he called it "The Law of the Universal Disproportion of Efficiency." Occasionally, with that brutality which somehow causes me to blush (which deeply displeases me for it makes me feel like a ridiculously naive little bourgeois), he affirmed that "the universe seems to be an enormous . . ." I do not dare formulate inferences nor draw conclusions, for I do not want the persons whom I respect to accuse me of blasphemy. However, I have always believed that Don Q spoke without malice: he deeply loved the Milky Way and he spoke with a slightly suspicious primitivism of the splendor and the beauty of the spheres and of the sacred lights that extend throughout Teuhtlampa. I believe that he loved God to an extent that I sometimes supposed was an elemental pantheism in which he himself identified with some integrating principle. Frequently I think that I should have avoided his conversation: it overwhelmed me, it irritated me, it surprised me, and I really can't say if I loved him, admired him, or if he infinitely annoyed me.

Here is one of his typical monologues which offended my civility, and yet, nevertheless, it pleases me to remember, in spite of his deeds, as nothing more than some unpleasant Hegelian implications.

"Is effort, in itself, an object of being?

"Is the game of opposites which negate themselves the motive of existence?

"Oh, the brutality of synergy!" (Always, when remembering these flippancies, I feel like not bothering to mention them.)

And he added, to complete the meaning of his famous law:

"How long is the road, devouring millions of spermatozoids for one fertilization!" (This rudeness has always bothered me. He could easily have employed some other simile without unpleasant implications.)

He continued:

"Is the way the sense? The result, what is it, in itself, but another contrary that is surely going to be negated by another force, though it might be only the force of time, that fruitful enfeebler?"

In comprehensible form he concluded as such:

"There is a law of the great equilibrium between squander and minimum wage. This is a natural law. Efficiency, the economy of result, is a human act, a daughter of reason." And with his great sufficiency he added: "Is that great amender, reason, the great rectifier of universal squander, or a simple transitory miser ('transitory miser'! What an idea!) against the universality of generous squander which penetrates all and transforms everything to fill the inexhaustible purse of possibilities?"

To fill the inexhaustible! A great parenthesis falls here: (I have always believed—and I never talked about it with Don Q, for he surely would have been most envious—that the Word has what I would dare call a diabolical freedom; it is enough to merely gather meanings to create absurd, ridiculous, unthinkable concepts: poetry, pure philosophy, or a whole universe, antiuniverse, or whatever.*

If God created Logos, the devil gave it liberty. The devil? It's a shame that I can't ask Don Q, nor dazzle him with that discovery about the diabolical freedom of the Word. May all this be on record because Don Q himself used to talk about "filling the inexhaustible purse." A few mean-

* The influence of the word-making machine patented by Don Q's uncle, Don Miguel de Unamuno, cannot be denied. (Author's note.)

ings were gathered, and the result was an expression, full of suggestions, that does not resist the slightest logical analysis. What bothers me most is that I somehow understand "filling the inexhaustible purse of possibilities." I think that that bag, if it exists somewhere, must have the form of a spherical galaxy. I close parenthesis).

Linked to his Law of the Universal Disproportion of Efficiency, Don Q would sometimes tell me:

"We always come to the mystery of the individual. The individual himself is an evident result of efficiency, although he might be a nest of contradictions. It is the only efficient limit of the infinite, although in time it may have an end. When you get to the individual you are on firm ground; you cannot break it in halves, for this would deny him. The individual may have been God's greatest hardship."

Does anyone understand what this means? On the other hand, it bothered me that Don Q spoke in analogies. It can't be denied that he probably was, more than anything, a poet: "nest of contradictions," "firm ground," "blessing of the limit."

I firmly believe that the great, and probably only, preoccupation for Don Q was existence. I don't know if I can call him an "I-ist" or "egoist." Both probably, in spite of his generosity. I believe that his generosity recognized the terrible vanity of the flowing fountain. On giving of himself, he affirmed what he called with great brutality "the majesty of the I." He dared affirm that the respect of the I's inferiority would be the Creator's greatest responsibility, if this were a personal one. How crude! And he added, in a tone that is almost blasphemous, "The dignity of divinity can only be understood in terms of an untransferable I."

His great desire was to know if the I persists after it is

created. He did not discover any essential argument. Not even the one about majesty or the one about dignity. One of the most terrible doubts that he passed on to me (and I believe that I hate him for it) is the argument about the necessary mortality of the I in order to avoid identification with the divinity. He called this principle "the I's annihilating necessity against the persistence of the infinitely imperfect being."

Occasionally he formulated a simile, rather more geometric than poetic. He told me, with a sneer of deep satisfaction, that the I was a simple position in the infinite, a point that would become a dash in time and a body in space, and that, together, they made the universal screen, a shadow pantomime of the boredom of some god. (He said this about God, but I didn't dare transcribe it. I don't know why I'm afraid to do so, for I believe that my freedom gives me the right to do so, if there is respect in the intention. That's why I opened this parenthesis.)

Abusing the simile, he came to say that the dash generated by a point had to be finite: otherwise, each dash would convert into a spherical universe, turning on its center and later on its diameter, and all the dashes would be confounded, and with that would come the end of the great amusement. I ask myself if this impressive argument of chilling geometric similitudes makes sense.

He called that thesis "the genetic property of dynamic Ieity." Yes, that's what he called it, nothing less.

Explaining the doctrine, he reasoned: "It is enough that the infinite exists to conceive in it any position that is a conventional point. It is enough that the point occurs in time for it to become a line; it is enough that a line turns on its center or persists for it to generate a surface, and we are already in space, departing from time. It is enough that a surface occurs in time and that it displaces itself in space to form a body. It is enough to move a body in time and in space to arrive at the magnificent incomprehension of God." The wretch was so serious! And afterwards he said, "Substitute the I for the point and you will begin not to understand the Creation."

I think he meditated too much. He projected his "Ieity" for hours (I believe that with this expression he joined the words "I" and "deity" into what he called "dynamic ability to propose oneself as a motive of meditation." And I think he added "transcendent meditation.")

Ah! For he certainly was a deeply transcendent fellow. He used to say that the only possible transcendence of the I is God. Therefore, I believe, his meditations about "Ieity." Ieity!

Occasionally . . . What did he say to me occasionally? Oh yes! It was something which impressed me greatly because it was manifestly incomprehensible. He told me (let's see if I remember it), something like "that the quantity . . ." Now I know: that the infinite was quantitative, although necessarily spheric, but reversible starting from an eye or a navel that was in all quantifiable points of a sphere in infinite reverse. And what a good example our universe was: whichever point one approaches, one contemplates spheres similar to the first, like soap bubbles (I thought of this simile to unexplain the idea), which grow equally to the outside and to the inside, and towards all the paths of the sphere at the same time, equally as large as small. And what's more, repeating the phenomenon in every sphere!

Because I told him that I didn't understand a thing, he told me that it couldn't be explained with words but only with music. He tried to reproduce symphonic passages by Beethoven with a reed flute. I don't know whether it was the Fifth or the Ninth. It might have been a quartet or a sonata. Anyway, I didn't understand what he told me nor what he played for me. He insisted (playing the flute and speaking at the same time!) on the "infinite progression of the unfolding of the spheres that withdraw over themselves." He thereupon concluded, I don't know why, that the infinite was necessarily temporal, or that time was conveniently spherical and particularly unfolding! (What an idea!)

CHAPTER II: *Concerning "Ieity," the Infinite's Navel, the Sphericity of the Logos, Music's Rotundity, the Wind, Darkness, and Other Important Details About the Loss of Memory, Hermetic Plenitude, and the Eternity of the Logos and the Solitude of the World.*

WHEN I told him I didn't understand his words, he responded smilingly:

"My dear Pepe" (when he called me "my dear Pepe" with that protective tone, I think he was either making fun of me or he despised me heartily). "My dear Pepe, listen to my words as you would music. That's why I speak them through this reed flute.

"There are times," he added, "in which the Logos is only music. Don't try to understand it in a linear sense, enjoy it in its spheric plenitude. In essence, the Logos is not made up of one and another word that are combined while each retains its own sense. No. No. The Logos is a spheric totality that you should enjoy as music; it is a sphere that integrates itself into time. Wait until the time of the Logos occurs so that you can enjoy it in its complete sphericity. Otherwise you are confusing the beads with the rosary."

"Don't let time make you its slave," he would tell me. "Yes, it will make you old, but do not let it overcome you. Do not let transitoriness overcome you. Seize the spheric sense of things, especially Logos and music. Defeat them with your memory's spheric plenitude." (One can't help but recognize that the fellow was proud.)

"Memory," he would tell me, "is anti-time. It's a more intelligent resource than intelligence. Who knows who first thought of giving being memory? But the I appeared at the moment when memory appeared. The rest was only a problem of pride and some other things. In this way one arrived at 'Ieity.'

"Take advantage of your own memory while you have it, because when you lose it, you will forget about yourself." (While saying this he puffed like a hurricane that carries everything in the darkness. At the end he almost screamed, "*Yohali Ehecatl!* Wind and darkness!")

"Take advantage of your memory to seize the full spherical unity of music so that the notes don't drip one by one, sacrificed to the transitory; expect to receive all of them and remember all of them. Then the Logos will inundate you in all its plenitude and you will have made fun of that generous doter which is time."

(Naturally, he repeated certain expressions which I believe he had fallen in love with: for example, the one about the "generous doter." He repeated it, giving special sonority to the combination of the strong "r" and the soft "d". I have the impression that he effectively enjoyed words as well as music and that the former gave him special delight. He repeated them many times and not only would he say them and hear them, I suppose he thought them, and, what's more, he relished them. I think they tasted to him like something. I'm not mistaken in that thought. It is indicated to me by the fact that he lived each instant and each detail with all his senses so that somehow they would seize something.

For example, words. Apparently they provided him an intellectual satisfaction if he spoke them dialectically. They flattered his memory when they arrived conveniently to it; besides, he said them loudly and, when they pleased him, not only did they become music, he tasted them, he swallowed them, and many times he digested them! I am making this parenthesis too long—I'm abusing my rights!—but once and for all I would like to clarify this matter of words. His intelligence, he used to say, captured them in their spherical totality. When he seized that totality he called it "Logos." "I'm in the eternal hermetic plenitude of the Logos," he used to tell me. Logos, Logos, Logos! He tasted the word. The Logos is permanent. It doesn't occur, nor does it strictly require memory, for it is the outcome of the reciprocal annihilation of time and memory.)

"It is," he continued, "total thought and it comes out after it has been articulated, when it no longer needs the word-drip or memory to retain it anymore. It is total thought, quiet, full, and eternal. It is, perhaps, the form in which the learned, not the saints, want to understand God. Logos, Logos, Logos."

Nor did he scorn words because of that. Words, words. No. He lived words, occasionally with delight, sometimes with pain. Although, it is evident, he was indifferent to many. At every moment he thought about words. "Yes, they are," he would say, "in the flow of time. Each word, each meaning, in itself loose and incomplete, has an insufficient beauty of its own, destined to combine with others to gain the right to Logos. Until words arrive at Logos they are single, imperfect penitents who cry in the Vale of Tears with their sights set on their final condemnation. Words look too much like me. They have the same false plenitude. They are the fallacious transitoriness that aspires to Logos, like saints and madmen who aspire to heaven."

"The word," he once said, when I wanted him to establish certain distinctions (undoubtedly I'm a bad candidate for a scholar), "is another thing. The word is will, responsibility, behavior. With it we are saved or condemned. The word is a unique, an intimate responsibility of man." And he would tell me in a dramatic tone, which I hope was sincere: "The word is man's ultimate solitude! It is the suitable universe of his will and conduct. Man is good or bad through the word. The word is the carrying-out, the what-to-do, the must-do. The I's only compromise is with its deity. Through the word, man is alone against himself, free from God, alone, alone, demoniacally alone!"

CHAPTER III: *A Parenthesis About the Fascination of Words, and the One Which Is the Most Beautiful.*

(YES. He liked words for their sound, for their representation, and for their meaning. When these three things were combined, the three sensual pleasures of words, he was almost happy. I suppose that the word that pleased him most was an Indian, Nahuatl, word. That word was "teuhtlampa": Teu-h-tlam-pa . . . Teu-h-tlam-pa . . . Mysterious, musical, delicious, beautiful. I think it means firmament, in the sense the spheres extend through it and the gods inhabit or pass through it. It fascinated him to hear and say it: Teuhtlampa. To think of it. To enjoy it: Teuhtlampa. It pleased him in its dry solitude. But, qualified by Castilian, it also pleased him as a mestizo product: "immensity of Teuhtlampa," "profundity of Teuhtlampa," "the infinite Teuhtlampa." "It's the most beautiful word that the human throat has invented," he confided to me, and added, "Fortunately its supreme musical beauty corresponds to its representation. I understood it," he told me, "one night when I was in bed with my head towards Teuhtlampa, my back solidly resting on the Earth's curvature,* lovingly glued to its solidity, confident and quiet. I saw the stars—another beautiful word—the elongated and sovereign mark of the Milky Way, the cold depth of darkness, and suddenly, by looking deeper, a steady vibration came to me from all the immense depth of Teuhtlampa, the presence of the universe, the meaning of the stars, many, many more than the ones I was seeing, more, many more in the darkness. They were a presence, they were a present, quiet music made of spheres and galaxies, with which I took communion lying down on my dear ground. And I was humble and proud. I was shadow, cloud, light, and darkness. I was in the middle of all things; I was someone in the unfathomable immensity. I was a quiet point that referred to a system that penetrated me, and that, in its equilibrium, allowed me to enjoy the curve of my ground with my back, my eyes, and my skin. The deep, vibrant immensity of Teuhtlampa. It was a beautiful night," he told me confidentially, "one of the most beautiful nights I have spent in my life. In time I will tell you of others that can be told." And he concluded: "If the sound and the representation of Teuhtlampa corre-

* Antoine de Saint-Exupéry, Don Q's cousin, had a similar experience. (Author's note.)

spond to its beauty, the meaning, in its plenitude, approaches the Logos and is almost God."

And thus he justified his preference. I thought about whether I knew a more beautiful word, and had to answer that I hadn't even thought about the beauty of words, and even less about the most beautiful. In my admitted mediocrity, which imposes itself on me before Don Q's determination, I think with humility that I have not arrived at the condition necessary for determining the most beautiful word. I analyze many, and, before concluding anything, the enterprise seems stupid and I remain undecided. What do I care which word is the most beautiful? Nevertheless, I think it is good that someone has the time to ponder these unnecessary questions. Which word is the most beautiful that you know? I now close the parenthesis.)

CHAPTER IV: *About the Crates of Green Worms, the Dynamic Property of Proposing Oneself to Oneself as a Motive for Reflection, and More Excesses About Memory.*

IF I remember correctly, before this excessive parenthesis, we were talking about memory. It was a long parenthesis to give Don Q's sensibility credibility. He probably was, I strongly insist, more than anything, a transcendent poet. He frequently mistook beauty for truth. Stuck to a beautiful clue, he preached his discovery as if it were true, he held on to aesthetic considerations as if they were ontological or logical or dialectical. It was odd to study him in his moments of "penetration" as he called them. I believe the greater part of his absurd mistakes derived precisely from the fact that he never decided to look only for beauty or only for truth, at least not at the same time. When I told him this observation, he looked at me with sadness and said:

"You belong to the gravedigger type. You like to crate and bury everything, in the ground or in drawers, it doesn't matter where. When you open your dirty drawers, you are going to find them full of purple, viscous, greenish worms. What the hell do I care if what happens to me is aesthetical, ethical, or ontological? It simply occurs to me. I hate worms, the same worms that your brains are going to become in a horrible viscous ruling passion enclosed in your cranium's box."

How odd, I thought—without knowing why—that I'm able to think with my brains, that some day these same brains are going to turn into worms, and, unwittingly, I became aware that I was indulging in what, as I already said, Don Q called "the dynamic property of proposing oneself to oneself as a motive for reflection." I didn't dare tell him this, for he would have immediately drawn some unpleasant conclusions. But I remained with the restlessness of imagining my skull full of worms, or worse, pestilence. I believe that these are the topics of meditation hermits propose for themselves. It can't be denied that they are most unpleasant themes. Precisely because of these suggestions I used to flee from Don Q's presence, which, I must say, I couldn't take for long. At the least, he tired me.

This thing about memory I believe to be very important. Don't you think so? I don't believe it is Don Q's discovery. He probably read it somewhere and then tried to impress me. Memory! Memory is the anti-time! He is right, I think. What would my responsibility be without my memory?

Could I sin or repent? (How easy it is to act like Don Q and to go on, on my own.) Actually, memory allows living in the present, becoming aware of what is present, and annihilating what is passing on. Of course! Now I understand why one day Don Q told me:

"The inert stone is to sculpture what memory is to music. The substance of music is memory, much more than sound, which is a simple pretext. What would there be if we couldn't remember? What would we be if we didn't know what it is we know, or what it is we don't know?"

"My Ieity," Don Q used to say, "is memory and will." And he told me, and, although I tried to forget, I have just remembered it, "Whoever God is, he needs someone to remember him, that's why he created men." He added, "He gave them memory to exist, will to conduct themselves, and freedom to forget him. Will and freedom are linked to each other, essentially they are the same thing. When you think of them as one thing, it's called 'res-pon-si-bi-li-ty.' " (He used to break up the syllables in this word in an irritating way, as irritating as his "almost-moral" look at the time.)

In regard to this famous responsibility, he used to say many things that I will try to remember for a propitious occasion.

What I really remained convinced of was the problem of what a great thing memory is. Imagine a world without memory. Impossible! Because—and this is a conclusion that Don Q surely must have drawn from something he told me—it is impossible; because imagination is memory backwards, projected to the future, negating, at least partially, what happens. "Memory and imagination," Don Q told me, "are the great absorbers of time, past and future. What's more, without them there would be no present. Everything would be an antimony, which would make my

Ieity impossible." In an openly offensive way, he added aggressively, "And even the grayish aridity of your solemn bachelor's degree would be impossible, your ridiculous I, my dear Pepe Seco."

For a reason I choose to ignore, and although I'm certain he enjoyed having these dialogues with me, my personality bothered him deeply: my age, the bags under my eyes, my lack of hair, particularly my professional degree. He could not stand the fact that I was a Bachelor of Law from the Universidad Nacional Autonóma de México.

Whenever he could, and even when he couldn't, for example when a conversation theme was exhausted, he would say to me in various, but always deprecatory tones, "Well, my dear Bachelor Pepe Seco." Or, "So this is the great Bachelor Pepe Seco," or other expressions of that kind which I would rather not remember for they are manifestly unpleasant. Besides, this is something of little interest.

CHAPTER V: *Concerning the Universal Saturation of Infinites, the Generator of Time and Space, the Necessary Imperfection of the Infinite. With an Appendix Concerning March Rhythms and the Total Captation of Our Wonderful and Blue, Round World.*

WHAT follows is rather interesting and, for a change (I suppose), has nothing to do with my professional title:

"There's a principle," Don Q once said to me, "that I call

the universal saturation of infinites and that explains, and makes possible, time as well as space. This can be better explained with a drawing." He drew it for me: a flat figure eight whose lower contours, and that of one of the circles, plunged uninterruptedly, like an arm which ended in a hand whose thumb and index finger remained above and below the top line of the eight. The same happened on the other side where the contours corresponded to two arms with two hands, one above, one below, with index fingers that held a sand clock whose center line also touched the top part of the corresponding eight. As you can see, an absolutely incomprehensible description. It had to be seen. I'm sure you didn't understand the drawing's description, as I'm sure you will not understand the oral description of what it tried to signify graphically, among other reasons because undoubtedly I didn't understand it either, and I have to trust my feeble memory and my slight understanding. In short, I will impart whatever I can, trusting that your capacity for comprehension will make up for my notorious inability to transmit information.

"From the time I first became aware of things, the mystery of time and space has disturbed me, dimensions that condition our existence like an elapse," Don Q began to explain with the profound seriousness with which he used to speak of his favorite themes. "An elapse is the best way to empty space in time through the principle of saturation I have told you about. It's the first limiting consequence," he added, "of the constant transformation of imperfect infinites. Things are different because they are imperfect; because they are different there is space, and because they transform themselves there is time. That's what I call," he added seriously, "the specific weight of imperfection, whose gravest defect is infinity, which is the total absence of the absolute."

"Don Q," I told him desperately, "I don't understand you at all!"

"Don't despair," he answered, "wait until I finish and you will see that I don't understand either. But it will interest you," he concluded with an enigmatic smile.

"Look," he told me, "wherever you may turn your head, wherever you explore, you will find something that has no end. Profundity is a constant and interminable possibility. What's bad is that the infinite is found in what is large, small, and what is in two halves. In this" (he separated his thumb and index finger) "as well as in this" (he separated both arms) "and in the earth's roundness" (he made a corresponding gesture). "The infinite fits anywhere. The very fact of having no end is everywhere. It is then that the principle of the saturation of infinites occurs. Here, there, over there" (he again made the appropriate gestures) "are infinites; you end up understanding that infinites saturate and overcome, and then space occurs and time elapses, all possible in view of the continuous saturation I speak to you about. There are moments and distances precisely because all infinites saturate. The thumb is as infinite as the index finger, like the space which separates them. They saturate, and then you can understand the finites.

"I don't understand exactly why," he added with an expression of extreme concentration, "but because the imperfect is infinite, you can slice it as in fact it constantly slices itself, and you then have conventional pieces of infinites with finite form and all. If I were a mathematician," he added seriously, "I am sure that I would find the saturation formula with which the universe would hand to me its greatest secret: the identity of the infinitely large and the infinitely small, in whose exact middle, man finds himself. I think we can find the saturation of great distances with this formula; with it we would also arrive at maximum acceleration so that we could still be located in any point of the universe. Some day, some place (a problem of time and space), someone will find techniques to apply the principle of the saturation of infinites. Maybe then that someone, if it's a man, is going to be so bored that he will have to create another combination."

I suspect that Don Q wasn't very convinced, or that he didn't at all understand what he said, or that he hadn't gotten to the gist of the matter, or didn't know how to explain it well enough for me. It's also possible that he did not understand it and therefore could not transmit it. I think we are limited containers that can only retain, and consequently we can transpose what literally fills us. That theme is evidently too much for me, and even for Don Q in his incredible pretension. You have to see Don Q's drawing. It never ceases to be irritating in its simplicity. Frankly, it's more comprehensible than what I've just finished telling you.

To this aim, Don Q always remembered one of Beethoven's expressions: "Music is a higher revelation than Philosophy." He insisted on, and even realized, an experiment in developing the same theme through different means of expression, especially letters, painting, and music. Although there were obvious agreements, there were themes that evidently were better expressed by one of these means of expression. I think he would have liked to be a polyphacetic artist in order to transpose from one art to another questions that mattered to him, in search of the perfect expression, which might be, he said, "the simultaneous seizing of the theme by all means of expression through the integral reception of all the senses." This came to him, he told me, during a night when he was descending from the Oaxaca Sierra to the Isthmus of Tehuantepec.

"I became aware of the nocturnal landscape," he told me, "with all my senses. It was another unforgettable night in my life. A complete night. I had hiked all day; night fell and a beautiful, at first rosy and later silvery, tropical moon came out. You ought to know, my dear Joseph, that the elementary rhythm of the march produces an almost hypnotic effect on me. After walking hours and hours, I end up floating; almost gravity-less, I unfold in my world, this beautiful blue sphere full of life, with all my happiness. I lose weight walking. Repeating again and again the one-two, held and invariable, which dissolves me into the environment, and I don't know if I end up in my skin or if my conscience englobes itself in the horizon. I don't exactly know what my limit is. I'm only aware of my conscience's center; I don't think, I only live and walk. One-two, one-two, one-two. That fall is interrupted by every step. The rhythmic knowledge of earth's gravity and the majesty of the step. How beautiful walking is! What a privilege! One-two, one-two. To unfold, to convert your muscles into landscapes. To feel the beating of your heart against the counter-rhythm of your step. One-two, one-two. To measure the roundness of the earth. To be planting and eradicating yourself with every step. I end up identifying with the environment.

"That night the rhythm of my step had hypnotized me in a very special way. So much so, that it became night and I continued to walk. It was then that all my senses brought, through their different channels, the same nocturnal theme: the moon, seen falling over the landscape, began to be like breath in the tropical fragrance; the fragrance became music in the Tehuantepec River's water, which was coming down from the highlands reflecting the moon's rays; its water caressed me warmly and softly when I had to wade in it; my own legs added notes to the river's song. Passing an enormous mango tree, I pulled a mango which was as round and fleshy as a breast. Eating it, I was eating the landscape. All at the same time, Joseph, everything, my sight, my ears, my skin, the scent, the flavor. Everything at the same time! The same theme expressed in a different way—but identified, integrated in that unforgettable night in which I felt, with the greatest and most savage joy, what it was to exist, to be young, to be strong, and to be able to walk to the rhythm that our round, wonderful world gives us."

CHAPTER VI: *How Don Q Descends from Teuhtlampa and Wherein the Tale of the Suicide Frustrated by a Host of Tricks Is Begun, in a Manner Similar to the Tale of the Good Pipe.*

FROM what I've just told, it will be understood that Don Q was not merely interested in Teuhtlampa's affairs and its surroundings; nor was he an exclusively transcendental fellow always engaged in the depths of the firmament or entangling himself at every step in or with the infinite. No. He also used to come down to earth, he loved life affectionately and was humane. He even knew how to be in the company of men.

"I haven't told you," he once told me, "how I was able to prevent a tortured youth from committing suicide. I employed a host of tricks. I will tell you these things as if they had occurred in a sequence comprehensible to you; more than comprehensible, which is not the word because these are simple things, I'll say a sequence familiar to you. They happened like this:

"I was listening to music, as I do every day at various hours. You should know that my life is full of music, I hear it with my ears, I see it with my eyes; some passages come directly to my thorax and some to what they call, I don't know why, the mouth of the stomach, and to other unmentionable parts. But these are frivolities. Let's get to the matter:

"It was night and it was raining with relative intensity. I like rain. I love it deeply. You know that I never protect myself from it. I'm not like you, wearing raincoat and hat. You never face it. I do. I like to see the gray clouds full of water, to imagine how they break. I raise my face trying to see the trajectory of the drop that is going to fall on my eye and slide down my cheeks. (What an ugly word, cheeks! It's a shame that other words for it are so shoddy.)"

(I open a parenthesis to make it known that Don Q baffled me with these out-of-character remarks. Forgive me for trying to reproduce his conversation. Be forewarned. For my part I will try not to interrupt. May the baffling—if it baffles you, because it may not run its own course. I close.)

"It was raining, I remember well that the rhythm of the rain interrupted Vivaldi's Concerto for Four Pianos. I didn't know which rhythm to resort to when thin Albert came home, with his cultivated, though unbearable, German looks. He was dripping water like a stray dog, he was panting like a dog. I think I even noticed irritation in his eyes, but more likely drops of water. What I did notice was that he was baffled, even pale. He extended his hand to greet me. It was a long bony hand that was a bit soft, one of those hands that one seems to wring when one shakes it. In this case they were cold and wet. Come, come! I thought. Rain wets all. Even the well-groomed Albert. I would never have imagined that the rain might wet him. I accepted the fact that his hand was cold and wet with all candor. I didn't even try to resist his yanking my hand, because he was so scared that I didn't want to bother freeing myself from it, as I had done other times when he was drunk. (His hands perspired whenever he drank beer; they were then humid and sticky. Unbearable!)"

(I am opening a parenthesis, forgive me. Why this preamble about music, rain, hands, etc.? He was trying to tell me how he saved a life with a host of tricks, and we still don't know the beginning. But that was Don Q: sometimes he only spoke of his Ieity, the wind, darkness, *Yoali-Ehecatl,* the most terrible name man has ever given to a divinity. We'll come back to this. But he was interminably detailed when he let loose about the things of this world. I continue to dare to bother you, just so you may have a complete idea of who this rarest of beings was who answered to the name of Don Q. I close.)

"Of course, this Albert," he continued, "was the son of a German man and a Mexican woman, but he cultivated openly the German type. He assumed, whenever he was able, intelligent attitudes. He had even mastered a polished expression of serious intelligence, especially when the person whom I will call Don Lu and I talked about our respective Ieities. But I will not bore you by talking a great deal about this thin, frequent drinker of beer. Certainly, he drank beer to give credibility to his Germanness. I remember him well: thin, thin, drinking and drinking. Whenever he got drunk, besides the perspiring of his hands, as I told you, he started to sing the flea song (I have the impression he had put music—I confess it wasn't too unpleasant—to the song that the happy companions sing in one of the first scenes of Goethe's *Faust*). Whenever he sang, simulating a bass, which was not at all natural because he frequently choked, it meant that he was soon going to vomit, which he did spontaneously and with great clamor."

(I open a parenthesis. And the suicide? The tricks? Had he forgotten them? I asked myself. But no, it continued as follows. I close.)

"On that occasion he was almost sober and his hands didn't perspire. He didn't sing at all, although he looked as if he were going to vomit. If I must be honest, I never liked thin Albert." (What do I care? I ask myself, though I never told him so, for it would have ended the conversation. Don Q was very sensitive.)

"He took my hand and told me, disturbed and without gargling the g's, which he used to g-g-gargle when he exercised his Germanness:

" 'Q,' (he didn't call me Don Q as you do. Then no one used to call me Don Q. I was simply Q, although I must clarify that, because of it, I was less involved with my Ieity).

" 'Q,' he told me, 'Lu' (he also didn't call Lu "don") 'is going to kill himself before twelve o'clock today. Neither Ugartechea nor I can convince him not to commit suicide. You have to go and convince him.' "

On this note Don Q opened a parenthesis to explain who Ugartechea was: "Obviously he was an authentic Basque, except that this one was as rough as a real rock of the Pyrenees. But I must tell you, he was very good."

(It is I who now open the parenthesis, for, shivering, I noticed that he was going to interrupt the tale about the suicide and the tricks to tell me about Ugartechea. To avoid writing that name, I'm simply going to call him "Ug." I think it will match his bruteness and simplicity. Whenever I use Ug here, it will be understood that Don Q said, slowly, tastefully, and with his whole mouth, "U-gar-te-chea." I close.) I continue with Don Q's parenthesis:

CHAPTER VII: *Something About Ug, the Belief in Creation, Logos, Words, and Literature Again. And Wherein the "Bread Legend" of an Anonymous Author of the First Third of the Twentieth Century Is Broken.*

"UG was very good. So that you may get an idea of how good he was, and also so that you may have some previous knowledge of the characters who figure in these simple matters I'm telling you. . . ."

(I open parenthesis. Why, I ask myself, did he emphasize simple matters, as if he were embarrassed to tell me things in his narrative that normally occur to mortals in life? It seems that it sufficed for him to speak of "abysmal or cosmic transcendalities," as he once called them, and I remember that I observed at the time the satisfaction he felt for words accented on the antepenultimate syllable. Once he even said "abysmal." I don't think it's worth it to continue to be preoccupied with these emphatic things. I close.)

". . . I will tell you the 'Bread Legend,' which this Ug inspired, just as it was received and interpreted by a contemporary chronicler."

He began in this way. (But first I open a parenthesis asking forgiveness for bothering you with these interruptions. I believe I have a right to express my doubts and to formulate observations. With true terror I advise, and of course maintain the fear, that Don Q will infringe upon us with a very long distraction from the main purpose of this tale. He is going to deceive us with the "Bread Legend" written by an anonymous chronicler. Why the eagerness, I say, to slow down the succinct, simple tale of the facts that motivated his decisive intervention and prevented a suicide with a host of tricks? Why doesn't he confine himself to what we prosecuting attorneys call a summation? I believe that deep inside he was embarrassed to deal with human facts rather than transcendental essences, and thus he diverted himself from concluding the tale, which, I am sure, will seem childish after so much circumlocution and parenthesis. Other times I have supposed Don Q pretended to dwell in the outskirts of the literary tale that, I don't know why, I believe he believed.

What an awkward expression: to believe that one believes. I never suggested to Don Q that theme, the belief in beliefs: "I believe you believe;" "I believe you used to believe," "You used to believe I believe." Moreover, I have to observe two things: that phonetically, the word "believe," to believe, is brutally primitive by not being guttural; I believe it was one of the first to be employed after the ones referring to primary necessities were agreed upon.

I have already forgotten the other thing that I must observe. I am making an effort to remember. Oh yes! believe [*creer*], is, at least in Castilian, very close to create [*crear*], which is also a primitive word. In all probability, belief [*creencia*] and creation [*creaciones*] are also very close: the creation of beliefs, the belief in creation. Don Q has neglected so many themes for meditation!

Now then, I continue my parenthesis. I believe that he believed literary creation to be the decomposition into circumstantial and irreducible moments of the tale's total sphere which the creator has *a priori* so as to make the theme primitively and originally his own. In other words, and don't believe that I myself think this; no, in one way or another I infer it from conversations with Don Q, I hold him responsible for all this. I'm too serious to give myself to these thoughts, at least spontaneously. So then I believe he believed literary creation consists in coagulating the existential [or possibly the existentiality of time?] into irreducible moments, proceeding contrariwise to how one arrives at Logos according to Don Q. Remember that Don Q believed that the elapsing of words must be awaited in order to achieve the spheric plenitude of Logos. In literature's case [and with this ends, astonishingly, the systematic analysis, Logos, word, verb, literature—which comes from letter] the creator departs from the total sphere . . . No, not sphere, something less transcendental: global knowledge, that's it, global. Global knowledge of the theme so as to decompose it, through the tale, into words attached to a recreated time, truly artificial, with which creation plays in a truly arbitrary form: "Once upon a time, many, many years ago, there was a good king who had three sons. . . ." These sons are born, grow, are all bad or vain except the youngest, they reproduce and die. But they live in a tale, and, somehow, in a permanent present, and they jump from one age to another, etc. See how literature is contrariwise to Logos? It decomposes the globe into the recreation of time. It recreates global existence in a successive series of artificial moments. In consequence, it is "transcendence backwards," as I'm certain Don Q would have phrased it. I believe these odd thoughts, for which I am not fully responsible, are encircling me; not to mention the influences that I do not always accept and that, against my will, I have received from Don Q—namely, Plato's main ideas and Aristotle's Entelechies. You don't believe it? Upon more thought, I believe that Don Q's influence came from something he once told me when we were discussing the problem of evolution. [I, from the scientific point of view, supported by Teilhard de Chardin's ideas, and he, from his absurd and peculiar point of view.] He told me:

"I am convinced, my dear Pepe Seco, that every culture, and what's more, every species, has a literary god." At that time I thought it was a purely poetic and frivolous expression. Now that the observation has ripened within me, as is evident, it seems that it was one of Don Q's more transcendental remarks, only backwards. I don't recall whether I need close parenthesis. I suppose so. I close.)

Continuing with our much-interrupted tale, I have the remote impression that we were up to what Don Q called, with his tendency to emphasize, the "Bread Legend," so as to illustrate either Ug's kindness or idiocy, I don't remember which, and to ascertain some of Don Lu's basic characteristics. It is, as you will soon see, a primitive tale, reiterative and candid, in a dubious style that can be attributed to the anonymous chroniclers of the first third of the twentieth century, still not sufficiently researched due to the great amount of accumulated material that would require a great amount of time to be classified, time in which, of course, more material will be accumulated, whence follows what a gigantic endeavor it is, which only future times will be able to undertake, and which, I am sure, will invent electronic paleontological machines to search through libraries and dumps for "the sublimation of intellectual and emotive misery of all time," whose geometric accumulation, Don Q believed, "overwhelms the sphere in which I whirl."

Here is the legend:

"He was a legendary man who did not even reincarnate into different bodies. He was the same body and soul that, unchanged, attended History's passing. Time stopped its march for that body and soul, and it changed them gradually into space and generation, always equal to themselves. He was the earth's son: he earned his bread by sweat, and the sweat even softened the mud of his lips. Yes, for it was the same man who then . . . And he prayed and gave thanks. For bread was given to him by Father Sun and Mother Earth, and he was good and was with God. And bread is a rich thing: it is also the earth's son and puts sun in our bodies. Because of it, the legendary man lives, and his body and his soul are the same ones as thousands and thousands of years ago. Not even History can take away from him the mud, which is still softened with sweat. He continues to thank Mother Earth for this gift, and the good God is content and his omnipotent hands bless the daily bread. And bread is sacred.

"That man was exactly like the man from earth you imagine who caresses with a plough and makes crackling ears of life grow in the earth, now like before, a long time ago, so long ago that not even he knows how long."

(A few more concepts follow here about tradition, the body, the soul, History's immobility, and God's blessing, which I omit with my indisputable transcriber's temper, for I think they are excessively literary and repetitious.) The tale continues thus:

"I will attempt to describe him to you (truly the man of the legend is what our Ug is), although you probably know him. He was rough, molded by Providence with blows, rough, very rough, but with an ancient distinction because he was very old, so old that he himself did not remember when he tore himself from a rock in the mountain. He had hands that were twice as large as mine, enormous, strong, rough, as must be the hands of one who takes fistfuls of dirt and kisses them.

"He was good, very good, so singularly good, so graciously good that many said he was a fool, very foolish. But I know he was good, with the simple and ingenuous kindness of long ago. I know he was good, because a child who loved me dearly and to whom I told many tales preferred him, without even knowing him, only because he held him in his enormous arms, and thus they remained without moving, probably very happy and well. Because he was good, he was very healthy and very strong and rough. He wasn't a fool, he was just simple, his body and soul unpierced by intelligence. His eyes weren't cold or designing, not even closed; he saw whatever he could through honest and loyal eyes, the eyes of long ago.

"He was good, simple, loyal, tolerant, he couldn't lie. He ate well and loved the land, the sun, animals, and children. He was, as I've said, rough, though distinguished, and he knew how to love and fight. He also knew how to cry, as I will tell you.

"But that man wasn't alone, and because of it, there was tragedy, a little tragedy in which no one died . . . that's probably why I tell it.

"No, he wasn't alone. There was also another one whom you undoubtedly know, he is the one who makes fun of the goodness which lasts thousands and thousands . . ."

(Herein are continued repetitive considerations of Goodness, Mephistopheles, purity, simplicity, envy, inferiority, destruction, scorn, and contempt, narrated with suspicious conviction by Don Q, who I think knew the anonymous chronicler. I don't reproduce them because they lack interest compared to the critical complications of our contemporary times.) I continue the narration:

". . . that friend and also I, the spectator who occasionally took the role of the chorus, were there.

"We ate and the old servant served us.

"The bread arrived and it was hard.

"The friend said, 'What filth! Stupid old lady! This bread is harder than your head and it's at least as old as you! Who decided to serve it to me? Just to bring it is to injure the softness of my palate!'

"He spoke and disdainfully threw the bread on the floor.

"The legendary man became pale and the fog of time veiled his eyes as he said, 'Don't throw bread! It is sacred!'

"The old servant departed, mumbling whatever an old servant mumbles in such cases. The good man picked up the bread and dusted it off with his enormous hands.

"Ridicule penetrated his friend's spirit:

" 'Don't be stupid or ridiculous! Bread! Bah! That filth made of land and full of sweat! Bosh! Sacred! Ha, ha, ha!' " (Exactly three times Don Q said "ha" in a truly Mephistophelian tone, like this: "Ha! Ha! Ha!") " 'Please! Don't be childish! Bread is your God's punishment since the time Eve, etc. . . . In order to eat it and throw it up later to make this thing called life, it eats dirt to come back to earth after standing on the land and resisting the sun. It's stupid! Sacred bread! Don't be a fool. Well, what do you think of bread which is so sacred that now it's a stone by virtue of being so much dirt. Forget it!' he said, and threw the bread again with even more disdain.

"The good man was now all legend, his body and mind were rolling from long ago towards an encounter with History.

"Pale in front of this sacrilege, yet tolerant of his simple knowledge, he picked up the bread again, dusted it off again and repeated, 'Don't throw bread! Bread is sacred!'

"But the other one, out of control, couldn't make fun of him.

"Imbecile! Jerk! I throw the bread because I feel like it! I throw it because I want to and I can! Now I throw it because you don't want me to throw it! I throw it because I shouldn't throw it! I throw it because, if it's sacred, I want to beat up the sacred and laugh at the sacred because it's so stupid! I throw it because I throw it!'

"He again threw the bread on the ground, this time with so much force that the hardened bread smashed into dust.

"The good man blushed. Mute and resigned, he picked up the powdered bread for a third time, but this time he didn't dust it off.

"He lowered his head, and, like an old Christ, two intense and silent tears fell from his eyes.

"The tears were falling from the furthest reaches of time.

"The enemy remained silent.

"And even I felt wicked.

"Tears oozed from his rough cheeks, until they fell to the dust which became mud. . . ."

That's how Don Q ended this tale, I must say he was moved. I see that it's odd that a character as complicated as he—who spoke of such important things, and who referred to universal pain with such seriousness (as we will see later), to the deaths of thousands, to failure and misery and hunger and other terrible things, without being touched—would be moved by a tale such as the one I have dared to tell you. For, logically, I gather I must identify Ug with the good and legendary man, and Don Lu with the destructive friend. I don't doubt it. I should have resisted telling the end of the tale, but I think it will be enlightening, due to something which I will soon relate. The tale really ended like this:

"Since then I have not heard anything about the legendary man. Maybe . . ."

CHAPTER VIII: *Concerning the Author's [Pepe's] Quasi-Solemn Scholasticism, and Wherein Continues the Tale of the Suicide Frustrated by a Host of Tricks, Together with Some Odd Information About Hail and the Conjunction of Principles Which Probably Ignore Themselves, and Other Excesses of Dialectical Integration.*

THAT'S how the tale really ended. In time I gradually learned, though I can't swear to it for it was only vaguely alluded to, that Ug, whom I will again call Ugartechea in this section, eventually married an extravagant and strange, rich woman who owned a hotel somewhere in Baja California, that he successfully managed the bar and slept in a hammock during the day, and that he was pampered by his wife, who, nonetheless, didn't give him any money. It is said that Ug then picked open the cashier's box. But I'm probably slandering him.

Don Q had completed one of his intermediate tales, but we still haven't made much progress in the tale of the suicide and the tricks. We have become stuck on the spines of our bristly conversations, and, I must confess, we have halted far too often because of my tendency towards parenthesis, which (for shame!) I sometimes fill with parentheses for lack of narrative means. Don Q once told me, regarding this tendency toward parenthesis:

"My dear bachelor," (whenever he called me "bachelor" without my name, he threatened me rather unpleasantly, and, as you will see, such was the case on that occasion.)

"My dear bachelor, the problem is that you suffer from a quasi-solemn scholasticism in your ill-fated and aggressive tendency towards distinctions and sub-distinctions which, not being able to fully explain, you decompose into parenthesis because, and this is the worst that can happen to a quasi-scholar, you're in a very precarious condition—with neither system nor transcendence—and therefore you have to be satisfied with the subproducts of my conversation. In other words, and to tell it to you with my most erudite disdain, you are a prospective, certainly mediocre, glosser."

Of course we won't stop to consider my character or to analyze the moving "Bread Legend." I have done enough extracting it from Don Q's narrative excesses with which was shown his thesis (or was it my parenthesis?) that literature consists of fabricating a very arbitrary dose of moments based on a global idea, distending the logistic (from Logos) *a priori* to later compress an artificial time.

I perceived an immediate and sudden conclusion of the narration. It was evident that Don Q wanted to depict a stupidly good character and a character strongly inclined towards evil's grandiloquence, its Mephistophelian style, although apparently very immediate and without many subtleties.

We already have three characters besides Don Q: Albert, Ug, and Don Lu. I think that's all we have perceived clearly in this increasingly complicated narrative process, in which, being conscious of what I was doing, I plunged to discover, or better said, to underline an almost innocent affirmation: that Don Q was not only interested in Tehuatlampa's affairs but also in human things, and that he was very humane. I should have simply said it and you would have believed my words. Instead, I wanted to give you an example which has taken me to unforeseeable limits.

Many pages ago we stopped where Don Q affirmed that

Ug was very good. I could have believed him, but I didn't have time to show him my faith in his words. Instead, he told me the "Bread Legend," which I told you about. We know then that Ug was very good and almost brutish, that neither he nor Albert could convince Don Lu not to commit suicide, as it was their intention to do before midnight of the day the complicated Don Q referred to.

"When Albert and I went outside," Don Q continued (I had already forgotten Albert's participation), "it was raining incessantly. As it was night, I couldn't see the grayish, paunchy clouds. Whenever I raised my face, all the drops which fell on it took me by surprise, for I couldn't see them because they were coming from the darkness. Added to the surprise, I felt a special sensitivity to the soft touch with which the drops came and decomposed their roundness, and to the way they slid down my neck to evaporate, further inside, from my body's warmth. They became warm in the trajectory." He continued:

"I have always been able to establish a precise relationship between water and my body. Haven't I told you," he asked me, "about my descent from Ajusco in the midst of a hailstorm?"

I had to confess that, no, he hadn't told me.

"I took off all my clothes except that which decency and hiking require; I put them on my back in a knapsack so as to have them dry later, and I started to descend, running down the Devil's Backbone." (I suppose the backbone must be a part of that mountain).

"The rather large hail beat me with some force and at first bounced on my head and body in a peculiar, reciprocal joy (the hail's happiness was evident, it was noticeable in the way it bounced). As it hit me I stopped feeling the impression of cold and became aware, through my skin, that hail is really drops of water, because a few stuck to my skin a while later. They fused in it and dripped with the same delicate gravity of an ordinary drop. Is it not strange, my dear Pepe, that what occurs in nature is due only to the conjunction of a few principles that must ignore themselves and a few circumstances that might coincide with themselves?"

I didn't understand the question, but as I had resolved to get through the tale of the frustrated suicide, I asked him what he meant.

"Sir, what a lack of comprehension! You are not aware of how wonderful it is to exist and to verify the encounter of principles that are autonomous among themselves yet destined to combine to create an infinity of effects, poetic ones among them?

"There's a principle that occurs in the paunch of clouds, by virtue of which these gaseous things either liquefy or solidify, and from their height, bang! they blindly precipitate to the surface, ignoring where they are going to fall. Keep in mind that they have to be prepared to fall on anything and to arrange an adequate behavior for each case, because it's evident that it's not the same to fall into the sea, on a rock, a leaf, or on a naked torso, don't you think so? And for each event they have a peculiar response, a behavior they either fuse or confuse themselves with, they either bounce or break. Add the additional problem of the angles of contact, which have their own laws. Raindrops are very important, but you're not aware of it. Have you seen rain on a sheet of water, in a puddle? Each drop gives off concentric waves that touch, include, react, crush, extend, agitate each other; others fall on top of them, spread to their limit, and there the effect dies, at least the one perceptible to my eyes, not my imagination.

"Once," Don Q added, "I thought that humanity was like that: a great reserve of cumulative water with a background of individual drops communicating from its center in interminable, incalculable combinations that arrive at and bounce against their comprehensible limits.

"When I imagined that, I thought I saw, better yet I resolved to see, the hands of men and women at the bottom of a puddle that held an apparently gray heart that evaporated and climbed towards the clouds, which were raining on each other.

"See how blind and barely transcendental you are. For you, rain is probably just another obstacle that you have to overcome on your way to work.

"I don't want to bore you, I see you're impatient, I see it in your slightly muddled eyes. You probably want me to reach quickly the suicide stage. Death, or its possibility, really moves you. Undoubtedly because it's important. The thing is, you don't know how to see every moment's death, the universal suicide of elapsing. In this case, the happy death of hail on my body. But contain yourself. The other principle, I will only speak of two among thousands, is a physiological principle; you probably know that when a strong body vigorously moves its muscles it generates heat. The same occurs if you rub ice. In each case, circulation is activated. Well, the effect of both principles, that of the hail and that of my body, produced an unexpected, totalizing result: in my joyous descent through the Devil's Backbone my body was letting off vapor, and it literally smoked between the hail and the mountain pines.

"It was a spectacle that I dare call extraordinary. And notice, only because two principles combined, without thinking about the precise result, they produced it as the most natural thing in the world. Isn't it extraordinary? Think about my body's heat modestly contributing to form the clouds from which hail fell and the hail, in turn, generated heat with its cold. Isn't it transcendental?"

This was precisely the squeaking type of transcendentality that I couldn't stand in Don Q, who looked for symbols, correspondences, and heights in everything.

I confess that upon hearing what I suppose was a personal anecdote, I became dumb, though I caught a glimpse of the curious spectacle: a naked man with a little bundle of clothing on his back jumping around the mountain and giving off smoke. If to that I add my conviction that that man was the great Don Q, the affair must really have been extraordinary, with total independence from autonomous principles and coincidental circumstances.

CHAPTER IX: *Concerning Elapse, the Universal Suicide, the Total Coincidence of All Circumstances, and Wherein Is Explored the Necessary Imperfection of the Infinite and the Insurmountable Differences Between the One and the Whole.*

DON Q certainly had peculiar expressions concerning circumstances and coincidences. He used to say, for example, exploring the previously mentioned theme of elapse, the universal suicide, that each circumstance was destined to coincide with every other circumstance of any given moment; otherwise elapse, the universal suicide, would be impossible because it would be enough to suppose that two circumstances did not coincide to understand the impossibility of that suicide which becomes necessary through the "law of imperfection's infinite generation."

"Everything has to elapse in everything so that everything may be exhausted and the infinite understood," Don Q used to say with disconcerting serenity, that serenity he assumed whenever he had the occasion to speak of the infinite or "infeenite" as he once said. Naturally I didn't understand him when he dealt with that question (I must acknowledge that it was not at the time when he was speaking of suicide but much earlier). I told him so, and he then elaborated the following, which we will call reasoning (I suppose you readers are totally resigned to one more interruption and a new parenthesis. This interruption has the advantage that it will deal with a connected theme, or better yet, one circumstantial to suicide).

"Once I told you," he told me, "that time is the generous doter. Go deep into the theme and you will find that, in the end, time is nothing more than the elapse of the imperfect towards its annihilation in search of perfection. If you really think about things," he added with an irritating finality, "we find that the universe, that is, the unity of diversity, is exclusively unified in imperfection, and therefore it elapses, because if it were perfect it would always have to be equal to itself, and, as there would be no variations, there would be no elapse, for time is the difference between two successive changes.

"Therefore, only the imperfect is temporal and it changes due to the necessity of its imperfection, for the imperfect can never be equal to itself. If it were, it would be the perfect imperfect, immobile in its own imperfection, which is a perfect contradiction. You will see why the infinite comes from the imperfect, which is the imperfect's aspiration to perfection, which to the former can only be accomplished through an infinite series of imperfect changes."

I should let it be known that when I heard him speak this judicious series of considerations, I clearly heard his brains squeak, as when an electronic sound system is drained by trying to reproduce itself.

I don't know if you're interested in continuing this squeaking theme. But I gather acquaintance with Don Q would not be complete if we did not continue to consider other questions related to this matter. I suppose someone is interested in these transcendalities. Unfortunately, for those who are not interested, I do not know exactly when and how Don Q will continue the tale. Therefore, I cannot advise skipping a few pages, or, least of all, that you stop reading them.

"Personally," Don Q said, neither narrating the rain affair nor the suicide but rather another theme, the one about imperfection's temporality, which, you remember, happened much earlier, "I have strong doubts about the infinite's perfection. I think that only the idea of totality provides us with perfection, but I find myself faced with a serious obstacle." (He used to say this with a frown and an air of great preoccupation.) "The irreducible, fundamental contradiction between the whole and the infinite results from the fact that the idea of totality is somehow limiting, while the infinite is not. Because of this, I think," he told me this with great effort and a tone of transcendental seriousness, "that the idea of the whole assimilates itself to individuality, and one and the other are contradictory limitations of the infinite's unlimitedness. In regard to that, I believe that Divinity's personal individuality would have to be total, but I find myself up against the problem of the contradiction with the infinite, and it repulses me not to give it infinity. Perhaps, if I substitute the idea of infinity for that of permanence, and permanence for that of immobility to make it temporal, I would understand this serious question. But that would take me to the necessity of a creative God, different from the created universe, from which the idea of totality suffers greatly."

(He looked genuinely disturbed whenever he used to say this, so much so that once I felt sorry for him. It seems that was the only point that occupied his mind and that he couldn't transcend. I say this because I believe that he couldn't have resolved all the problems of this truly Gordian knot of transcendentalities.)

These were truly obsessive themes for Don Q, who, I can assert, gave me the impression that he was continually and personally battling the infinite. I believe his passion for the Ieity came from this. He used to gladly take refuge in finite individuality for, he asserted, he was able to understand it "in its total indivisible unity." Whence his previously-mentioned multiple affirmations that the individual was the infinite's only efficient limit. He stopped at his own comprehensible individuality to oppose it to the infinite's monstrosity. From this, I believe, came that ever-frustrated effort to give Divinity a totalizing individuality.

CHAPTER X: *Concerning the One and the Whole As the Circle's Boundaries, and Critical Cases of Transcended Geometry As Problems of Thought Without Words.*

TO this purpose, I remember that he once confided in me with a truly Hindustani accent:

"The one and the whole contain the circle's only comprehensible limitation if you conceive of them as adjoining positions: a beginning and an end."

He remained silent for a while, and then he told me with profound disgust, "What's bad is that these two points, adjoining as you may conceive them, have to be conceived separately due to the infinite if I don't identify them." He added, "And if I identify them, besides committing a horrendous sacrilege, I again leave the circle limitless, which is the problem of transcended Geometry that I was trying to clarify." Then, truly exalted, he cried, "Now you probably understand why I have to seek refuge in the only fixed, indivisible, comprehensible, total point of my Ieity, inside the spherical infinite, which, by being central, as well as by definition, is indivisible. The trouble is that I have to give you and the others the same contradictory condition; actually to all those who are, have been, and will be, from which follows the timeless, spaceless indifference of these positions, which is notoriously at variance with History and Geography." Brooding, he remained silent, and left to listen to music.

I tell all this so that you may know what I had to suffer enduring Don Q's squeaks.

The only time I surprised him with a thought, one I'm aware of at least, was when, seeing him suffer what were grave questions to him (I talked to him because I'm a quiet fellow, conscious of my serious limitations, who tranquilly waits for death in order to continue ignoring everything with a resignation that Don Q never understood), I told him, using the formal form of address, of course:

"Listen, Don Q, I believe you are too enslaved by words. They are imperfect instruments, the fountain of your contradictions. Try not to think of words and you will probably find some tranquility. Your exaltation alarms me. It's going to harm your nervous system. You're as tense as a violin string (I am sure this simile pleased him), and because you are a huge resonance box (here I was being abusive), you enlarge every impression, and that can harm you." (He didn't thank me for my conclusion, I imagine because it could signify a protection he was never willing to accept.)

"You are right, José Guillermo." (The only time he used two of my three names. The other name with which I was baptized is Abel, but he didn't use it on the only occasion in which he had an opportunity to do so.) "You're so right, I believe I like music precisely because of that, because it makes me think without words."

(I can't do less than indicate that some time after this conversation occurred, he elaborated the theory, on which I have remarked, that he used to call "the transcendentalities of total words for the generation of Logos," a name I never liked because, I must say, it was long and employed the word "generation," which is equivocal. Of course, it's not that I want to attribute the merit of a theory, whose value I doubt, to myself. I make note of it only to contribute to the understanding of this peculiar character, for he never retained an affirmation which might interest him. He seized them as his own and made them grow, although occasionally he mistreated them lamentably. Some day I will give you an example of the latter action.)

CHAPTER XI: *Wherein Is Continued the Tale of the Frustrated Suicide and Don Lu Appears.*

A few pages ago we had reached the tale Don Q told me (I pick up the narrative thread where we left it, having played for a while with time, parenthesis, the infinite, and other details of this sort in order to accredit the arbitrary way in which Don Q played with the artificial time he was fabricating in his tale, I believe in order to accredit his literary possibilities):

"When Albert and I went out to the street," (you probably remember the former's visit to Don Q, etc., for we shouldn't repeat everything that happened up to this point. Etc. is better) "it continued to rain incessantly . . ." (Here follow thoughts about the surprising drops which fell from the darkness, etc.) What is important is to establish that "although it rained it was dark." I continue with Don Q's tale:

"The streets were wet and the strokes of lightning were reflected in the puddles multiplying their brilliant violent tone: later the roar of thunder was heard. . . ." (Don Q stopped here to amuse himself by considering the correspondence between light and sound.) "Some day," he told me, "a process to change thunder into lightning will be invented, because to me it's perfectly possible to convert sound into light." He went on and on about this point with fantastic affirmations to which I give no scientific value, therefore I do not relate them. Let thunder and lightning remain as poetic resources and not as doubtful scientific affairs.)

"I speak of lightning," Don Q had the discretion to pinpoint, "because one bolt caused the electrical current's interruption with which all the lamps went out." (Due to some odd primitivism he called public and domestic lighting "lamps.") "That explains why, upon arriving at Don Lu's relatively luxurious apartment, Don Lu and Ug were illuminating themselves with a beautiful wax candle that filled the air with its peculiar scent and created angles and conditions of illumination unusual in this century, giving an undeniably dramatic atmosphere. Imagine: rain, lightning, thunder, candlelight, and two touching faces—Ug and Don Lu, the latter a supposed suicide.

"I had been in that apartment, Don Lu's last gesture of prosperity, once before, but the candlelight changed all perspective and created mysterious corners, which the room's simplicity did not in any way deserve.

"When I entered, Ug stood up and, with the expression of a Saint Bernard in his eyes, looked at me with a sigh of relief, although with a convulsive grin of natural preoccupation. He told me nothing, I told him nothing. We only shook hands.

"Don Lu didn't even move. He remained with his elbows on the table, hands on his cheeks, staring at the candle whose light underlined the false wrinkles caused by his hands.

"I said nothing, I sat next to the table, also attracted by the light, which I stared into. . . ." (He went on with a long tale, too literary, about the wick, black and red at the tip; the flame's tones wavered from blue to green, yellow, almost orange, until they decomposed in the smoke's gray; considerations of the solid and liquid states of wax, something about refraction phenomena and color symbolism, which, except for the last, are worthless to relate. We will probably talk about symbolism later on.)

"We four were silent for about half an hour, sitting around the table, watching how light was nourished by the candle. . . ." (Here followed some associative thought about bees, honey, and light, which may be a part of Don Q's poetic expressions, but which, unfortunately, I've forgotten.)

"An almost instantaneous recurrence of electric current, followed by a new interruption, momentarily restored our century's normal sight and left the candle's flame converted into a mere anecdote on the table and not as the center it had been and would return to be. That interruption broke the near-hypnosis we were in, which allowed me to relate:

" 'Well, I know the approximate hour of the affair. What I don't know and am curious to find out is how, where, and with what it is going to happen.'

"Don Lu raised his head and looked at me with a look of irritation and disdain, almost with the same look with which dead people must watch some 'well-heeled' buddy say some intemperance that breaks the drama of the moment.

" 'I insist on seeing the preparations!' I said in an imperative tone, and added, 'Since I'm going to be the godfather in this affair, I have a right to contemplate the artistic aspect of the matter!'

"Don Lu stood up, furious. You must have understood," Don Q clarified, "the strategic aspect of my elementary intervention, which gave fruit to more than I had hoped, given Don Lu's subtlety, whom I had surely caught unaware and out of form, which was explainable given the constant contact I had recently had with Albert's 'beery Germanness' (what a daring neologism!) and Ug's inoffensive animality.

"Furious, he said, 'Get away, Don Q! This is my own affair and the affair of this pair of imbeciles!' (The imbeciles were very flattered by the legitimate recognition of their participation in an affair of such great significance.)

"He became aware that he had fallen into a trap when, with all tranquility, I retorted:

" 'Ah! Anger as prolegomenon' (I used this expression, precisely the shocking expression I had heard from you, my dear Pepe, when you were speaking to me of logic). 'Anger as prolegomenon, the scorpion's suicidal resource. It is not the normal state of a supposed suicide who leaves this life out of boredom.'

"He understood he had fallen into my trap and disdainfully he said:

" 'Subtleties!'—and again sat and stared at the light without looking at me.

"Ug took advantage of the incident to call me aside. I saw his reddened 'good dog' eyes, as if they had been crying. (I imagined some particularly dramatic scene set up Don Lu to destroy Ug and alarm Albert's phlegmatic nature.)

" 'Q,' he told me, 'don't be like that! How can you make fun of such a thing? Think that Lu will soon kill himself. He resolved to do so after we had left his father's house carrying the coin collection. He has no money now. He even fainted twice talking to me about what I had to do after his death.'

" 'But,' I told him," (remember what Don Q was talking about?) " 'Why is he going to kill himself?'

" 'He told me a long time ago that he could only live as a master and that the moment his life stopped being so and he would be forced to do the same idiocies as "collected nobodies," he was not going to give in.'

" 'And how is he going to kill himself?'

" 'I don't know exactly; he told me like Petronius that I should be ready to speak with him until the end, for he would be telling me his impressions. He told Albert the same thing,' he humbly added.

"Don Lu had gotten up and was able to hear Ug's last response. He looked at my eyes and asked, 'Any objection? Does it seem vulgar to you?'

" 'No!' I answered him. 'It just seems rather slow and too spectacular for your two little dogs. I think they're going to die before you, one by barking, the other from delirium tremens, sooner or later.' (You should understand, my dear Pepe, that I had made a point, for I had opened the possibility of dialogue and Don Lu was already facing the anticipation of death, the judgment of his form, which he must have thought about for a long time.)"

(I was surprised by the keen psychological strategy which Don Q was developing.)

" 'Go on! That's our affair. And you, what did you come for?'

" 'Man!' I retorted, 'First, to make a feeble attempt so that you don't kill yourself, and also because Albert asked me to. If I don't succeed, then to relate this spectacle to posterity, for obviously your happy companions are not artistic chroniclers."

(I open a parenthesis. I believe the dialogue more or less occurred in this way. Don Q used to be grandiloquent and he handled adjectives, adverbs, even adverbial phrases well, although syntax not so successfully. Of course the dialogue may seem conventional. It is not impossible that I might be improving it by not relying too much on memory.)

"Don Lu responded" (Don Q continued to narrate), " 'You continue with your subtleties and provocations in a discussion that I will not stand. I'd rather hasten my death. Soon you will start with your deep profundities and I will die either of boredom or desperation.'

"Playing the fool, Albert added, 'Then it would be an assassination.'

"I thanked him for his observation because it lowered the tension and gave room for some commentary. Ug, who didn't understand the situation, was in charge of this and said, 'I don't know how you can play like that with a man's life. You are frivolous. You even make fun of death. Don't you see, death is very important!'

"Albert followed with his German humor, 'Of course, none of us have ever died!' and he laughed slowly as if he were a full-bellied German—Ho! Ho!—and not a skinny wisp of a German.

"I thought it opportune to intervene with some expression that would be within the limits of subtlety and depth," Don Q went on, "so as to irritate Don Lu more. I told him:

" 'He who is almost dead is our happy companion Don Lu. He elapses now, slowly, towards the great gray buzz that death is. He touches the razor's edge; he feels the desperation of leaving the comfortable warm refuge of a healthy body; he anticipates the quivering of worms in his eyes' sockets and in his palate the muddy flavor of dirt swallowed without saliva in a premature communion it doesn't deserve!"

CHAPTER XII: *Wherein I Open a Parenthesis to Treat the Rights of Narration and the Scandalous Principle of "Transformity" by Means of the Artificial Generation of Time.*

(I'M sure no one is capable of imparting one of these characteristic phrases without blushing. Nevertheless I'm forced to believe what Don Q said he told me he said. I must confess I did not have the willpower to remain silent, and I expressed to Don Q my serious doubts that he, in a moment like that, would have had the tranquillity to construct phrases and figures like the ones he used. Don Q looked at me, I don't know whether with disgust or scorn, and said:

"Look, Pepete, narration has rights acquired from the time man stopped being a beast with his snout stuck to the ground. What matters are the situations man perceives, not merely what was expressed in them, but rather what he tried to say, what could have been said, what should have been said, and above all, what deserved to be said, so as to be at the level of art that is basically cultivated expression.

"To the narrator," he added, "events are like the stone to a sculptor. You have the complete right to draw your own consequences and to express them as it pleases your vanity, your own self-esteem, or your true vocation to stir others. I have already told you that literature is the great creator of artificial times that one builds and transmits to others, to the rest, in order to alienate oneself by projecting one's emotions."

"That pretension," Don Q further added, "I call the 'Principle of "transformity" by means of the artificial generation of time.' " [The expression is rigorously literal.] "In essence the tale, as an artificial manifestation different from nature, by being the daughter of one's intention and will, is a form of practicing love or hate." [He told me what name he gave to the principle implicit in that affirmation, but, probably fortunately, I have forgotten it. Perhaps I will remember it later. It was something like the "self-annihilating equivalent alienation by means of hate and love," only more complicated.]

"Besides," Don Q continued, "after having made me a victim of his emotional 'transformity' or however he might have said it, what I'm telling you happened just as I tell you it happened. You would have to understand the relation between Don Lu and me.

"Now, if it bothers you, I can look for the anonymous chronicler's version or imagine Ug's conversation in order to continue the tale, which I beg you to stop interrupting."

Still inside this parenthesis, which, be it known, I have

not abused lately, I must point out something you undoubtedly already have observed: Don Q's apparent tendency to continually instruct me. Don't be misled by appearances. It is not that Don Q wanted to give me lessons, it was simply his way of researching his transcendentalities. Otherwise he would have been alienated. I consider it an outlet and do not accept it as the constant didactic exercise that, of course, my pride and vanity would have rejected. I do not know to what degree the modern technicians of the tale may accept Don Q's resources. I simply transcribe them, expurgating, as far as I may, excessive roughness. I would have been more direct if I were Don Q. I wouldn't have thought of so many unpleasant delicacies [like rotten cheese, I say]. I would have been more direct. But in this and other things I recognize my limitations. However, if I were to deny Don Q's claimed right to say what he thinks about a situation, I would have to do it with a case that would have importance and power. Homes, for example, who could sing his "Oh, cruelest chronicle! What words thou uttered!" And of course we would not have had to do without this other example: "To be or not to be, that is the question . . ." and other monologues by the Bard of Avon who, it must be admitted, can in no way be compared to Don Q. Having these antecedents, I beg you to be tolerant with Don Q. Of course, the long parenthesis will deprive Don Lu's answer of dramatic effect. Just imagine it as being immediately after. That's all.)

CHAPTER XIII: *Concerning the Will to Reject Resemblance As a Notorious Contrast Between Don Lu and Rousseau, and the Luciferian Similarities of the Former, Beginning with Pride. Also Concerning Judas and Other Chilling Questions.*

" 'MANDRAKES!' Don Lu almost screamed at me." (Remember that Don Q's tale is herewith continued.) "Not even dead will I take communion with the earth. Neither with earth nor with anyone. I simply don't take communion. I don't admit anything in common, and if there were something in common, I would reject it with all my life. My compassionate Don Q, if that's life's order, I leave it to you. I so deeply hate equality that I love difference, my difference, which is love of myself and hate of my fellow men, to the measure that they are even that. I don't take communion even if they are my fellow men, for I don't admit similarities! I don't want fellow men!' "

"Listen, Don Q," I observed, "what a radical Don Lu was. He sounds too conventional, too anti-Christian to me. I especially don't understand," I added, "that business about loving himself and not loving similarities with others, for example self-love. I remember that the disheveled Rousseau founded society's existence and the qualities of general will on the recognition of a common love of self. Now you come along with this fellow, who was probably disheveled himself, founding hate of others on love of self and rejecting the similarity that can be born of the love each one has for himself. Isn't that odd Don Q? Isn't it too conventional?"

Although Don Q didn't like the Rousseau quote, with which I accredited my knowledge of political theory, he was satisfied with the intelligence of my question, for he gladly interrupted the tale to tell me:

"As a matter of fact Don Lu was, or is because I don't know what has become of him lately, an apparently rare fellow. But rare to the extent that he had sublimated a sentiment, better yet an attitude, that we all have to some degree: pride, which is a Luciferian way to solve the problems of Ieity."

I asked Don Q to explain this question further, which, honestly, seemed sufficiently suggestive to me.

"All right, Don Pepe," (the 'don' showed he was grateful for the opportunity to extend himself on a theme that interested him). "I will tell you a bit more about the Luciferian Don Lu: he had tried to solve the confrontation between the I and the infinite's imperfect anguish, rejecting all admission of its implications on his own will, which is the way through which, for loving a total and perfect God, Lucifer lost himself, by rejecting the creation made of stupid stones, vegetables which rot, worms that quiver, miserable men who hate each other, and all the other things that are in perpetual motion, undoing their imperfections to integrate time and its caducities. There's a great similarity between Lucifer and Judas that Theology has not explored. There is a voluntarily accepted dialectical fatality that makes both one, in the courage of accepting the condition to judge the Being's integrity, to admit it as imperfect and to protest; it is the presumption of having met and disliked God. These are things," Don Q had the humility to say, "that I say without fully understanding them, but I think they describe Lucifer as well as Judas. Due to that, by not understanding very well what I tell you, God will deeply love one and Jesus Christ will forgive the other, and he probably will want to love him some day in the universe and he will probably be seated at the right hand of the Son."

(I confess that these things give me chills. I don't know why Don Q dared to deal with these questions. Nothing was clear except my fear and perplexity. But as it was I who, on this occasion, introduced him to these thoughts, I had to beg him to continue the tale, which he did as follows:)

" 'You don't want fellow men,' I retorted," (Don Q is speaking to Don Lu) " 'and you say you are going to kill yourself, which ends in dying, one of the vulgarities that make us all equal. I believe, simply, that you are afraid. You have a horrible fear of asserting yourself in the world, and your fear doesn't accept the world's order. It's your fear of being too equal to others, too equal to me for example, too equal to Ug and even Albert. Deep within, it's a problem of pride.' "

("Notice," Don Q warned me, "that I was beginning to carry out the question by frankly attacking its Luciferian aspect, although I became aware," this confession by Don Q disturbed me greatly, "that I didn't want Don Lu's pride to lead him to suicide because it would have been an excessive test of my own pride, which would have suffered grave humiliation on proving that Don Lu, by being proud, would have killed himself, an act that my pride did not admit, with which I proved that I wasn't as proud as I thought I was and I justified my intervention in that odd case.")

"Don Lu remained silent for a moment while all of us contemplated how the candle was burning down. Ug asserted that it appeared to be crying. Literally, he said, 'I believe the candle is crying because it doesn't understand it is giving light,' an observation which," Don Q admitted, "amazed me in Ug, because I didn't understand exactly what I was doing there.

"A while later, Don Lu spoke slowly and quietly:

CHAPTER XIV: *More About Pride. Something About Paradise, Eve's Touch, and the Serpent.*

" 'YES,' he asserted, 'I'm proud. I realize I want to kill myself so as not to become like you or some other thinking imbecile full of quests and questions without answers, formulated whenever idleness allows it. Well, if we are going to please you, let's talk. I was going to do it with these two good friends, so different from me. If I could, I would ask their forgiveness for my disdain and for enduring me, because they accept me as I am.'

" 'That's a way to love your fellow men,' I told Don Lu, 'which shows you are a poor, scared little animal in this corner of the world.'

" 'Of course,' Ug said, 'we are accustomed to being together. Lu can't be without us, frightening or amazing us with the things he tells us or he imagines, and we love him. At least I love him, I don't know about Albert. I get along well with Lu, we travel and have fun together. We buy good clothing, go out, things like that. It's a shame he doesn't have any money. I'm going to have to work again. I will have to go back to my uncle's store and work behind the counter again. A kilo of potatoes, not enough change, things like that. There's no other way, it's my life. What I'm sorry about is that Lu is going to kill himself. I tell him not to, that together we will set up a little business, a business in . . .'

" 'Shut up, you imbecile!' Lu interrupted him. 'Leave those idiocies for when you're with your uncle or whomever, but don't let me hear you. Business! Business! What the hell do I care about your potatoes and counters. I've told you a thousand times that I don't believe in the slavery of work. No one can punish me. And look, Q, maybe you can understand me: I should never have left Paradise. And if something or someone comes to force me to "do business" in order to live, or to scrape my elbows on some counter, or sweat my ass off on a chair, or drag my feet on the street, I'll tell him to go to hell, or I'll go to hell myself and peacefully leave this life. I can't stand another's damnations. Don't mention making bread with the sweat of my brow. To me, if nothing comes without my doing anything, I'll do nothing. I'd rather die. Lilies of the valley for me. Don't mention fleeing Paradise to me!'

"Albert was lucky that night, because with a truly Teutonic smile he commented, 'You were the serpent there.' He celebrated his witticism with an outburst of laughter.

" 'Of course, clown, he wasn't going to be Eve. In regard to the boorish Adam, you already know what I think of his type and of yours who descend from Cain's side, because that stupid Abel didn't even have sons. While it's up to me—and I have a right to my wishes or I'll kill myself—I will not get out of Paradise. It's a matter of principle: coiled around the tree, tempting Eve' (here Ug smiled for the first time that night) 'or with the apple in my mouth—I'll be damned if I like apples—I will not do what everyone else has to do to live. Either I get everything so that I can enjoy it as I deserve it, or they all can go to hell, or I'll go to hell. But I will not leave Paradise on my own free will. I don't want to! I don't want to, and that's that!' "

CHAPTER XV: *Concerning the Rights of Human Will. Things That Happen and Other Equally Respectable Affairs.*

DON Q opened a parenthesis here and told me:

"You will notice, my dear Pepe, that in his harshness and apparently slight subtlety Don Lu was presenting a very transcendental problem: the rights of human will, a theme that you, as a lawyer, naturally will not understand because it's not in the codes. Ulpian said nothing about this, nor did any other Roman jurist. You will not find any precedents, not even the latest Jurisprudence, or in similar theses: the rights of human will."

Because his citation of Ulpian bothered me, I don't know exactly why, I tried to answer him, "Listen Don Q, supposing that, not granting that . . ."

"Bachelor! Don't go on! There are few expressions I hate as much as the one you have just dared to utter. Oh, most petulant Pepe! What words you speak! 'Supposing that, granting that,' just legal sophistry to exploit the idiocy of judges. Please shut up!" I shut up and listened to Don Q, who told me:

"I'm firmly convinced that the will has rights because it is free. Something has to happen when a free man loves or stops loving. Accepts or rejects. That's how saints and demons are born and how suicidal people die."

"Come on, Q," I told him, "don't give me that, whatever happens happens, that's all. As Chesterton said, 'things happen.' "

"Certainly a good man, my friend," Don Q said, "but it is not enough that things happen. I am thinking of things that should occur or about ones that occur unjustly.

"This is one of the most important problems that can be created for the human will," Don Q insisted. "Full knowledge of it gives a transcendental sense to rebellion or resignation, which is not simple conformity, but rather solidarity or lack of it with the works of God. From there comes Lucifer or The Lord's Prayer."

I confess that it seemed extremely interesting that the suicide theme would take us to those religious questions with which I almost never bother. I asked Don Q to go on and he said:

"I convey these fears to you because they are part of the questions between Don Lu and myself. It was clearly created for me while hearing the second movement of Beethoven's Seventh Symphony. It always makes me cry whenever I hear it. It is, if you can notice it (which I doubt because you're old), resignation raised to the most sublime acceptance of the universal necessity for the Will of one God for the love of creation. You must remember that that prayer, the only one Jesus taught us, is really saying 'thy will be done,' which is not a powerless fatalism but rather the transubstantiation of freedom itself by voluntary subscription to God's Will, which is resignation's merit. Then there are other ways, such as the Luciferian one, no doubt just as great, but terrible rather than sublime. Not to resign but rather to deny creation's order, not to accept it because freedom allows judgment, which is its maximum excellence, because it allows us to be proud, which is comparison with God.

"Another problem is authority. Can free will do nothing more than renounce and reject and rebel, although it might go straight to hell where I don't know what happens?

"But the moment it has liberty, it renounces, protests, rejects. That's what is truly important: free will's tremendous responsibility. It either resigns itself or renounces; accepts or rejects. One way leads to sainthood and the other way to pride. If in each case there's an awareness that what's in play is the possibility itself of choosing deeply, and to the greatest degree, the force that Liberty itself has available against all of creation, and to the limit of the will itself.

"Of course, in this case the problem had not been set up so clearly; yet it was pivotal, and was the difference that separated Don Lu and me."

I really don't know—I think—whether an attempted suicide is the proper moment to establish these brutally disconcerting questions. I confess that Don Q took me by surprise when he revealed such a mystic aspect. I had the idea of remarking to him:

"Listen, Don Q, you're turning out to be quite a mystic, you worry about theological things . . ." To which he replied with a certain preoccupation:

"Look, Pepe, although your observation is one of incredible vulgarity, I must recognize that there are things that terrify me and this is one of them. If you want to, change the names of things so that my qualification as a mystic may vary.

"Don't call it God but Universal Order, Nature's Way, Dialectic Thought, or whatever you trench mouths feel like, the problem can be set up in many ways. The way I have expressed it was precisely the way the problem lay with Don Lu."

As this observation left me saddened, I did not reply at all. Don Q was able to continue:

CHAPTER XVI: *Wherein Thin Albert Falls Head Over Heels and Wherein Information Is Given on the Servitude of Friendship. Some Negative Considerations of Sweat; with the Treatment of the Great Broom Angel, and the Appearance of One of Goya's Witches.*

"THEN thin Albert spoke again and said in a festive tone:

" 'Ah, so now Lu turns out to be serpentine and tempting?'

"Ug slapped him in the middle of his chest, so hard that thin Albert fell head over heels with the chair and everything, while he told him in his most offended tone:

" 'Shut up, Skinny! Don't get involved with what you don't understand. Now that Q has arrived you feel more secure and you start with your jokes and clowning. Shut up or I'll . . . !'

" 'Hold it, Ug,' Lu screamed as if he were addressing his dog, 'Hold it! Albert is right. I fell into Don Q's trap and here I am talking about the same idiocies, except that I now turn out to be "serpentine and tempting." But that doesn't change the situation, because it repulses me to even be serpentine and tempting if I don't have the opportunity to continue being without more effort than existence gives me. I don't want to do things I dislike, routines I don't understand, greetings and gestures in which I have never participated. To wake up at a fixed hour, go to the same place to extend my hand to get the money I have earned and not the tribute I need because I feel like it and that I demand, if I want to, by means of lashes. Not my sweat's money but my excellency's money, money that . . .'

"Ug interrupted him at this moment with such a humble gesture that it must have opened heaven's doors for him:

" 'Lu, I have already told you that I will work alone; you will not change your life. I can handle myself, I can sweat, I can't lose anything sweating. You have told me many times that I'm a breadwinner. Let me pay for your life, your excellence, or whatever you want to call it. You know that I . . .'

" 'The resigned faithful servant is beginning to speak,' Don Lu began to say.

" 'Or the good friend,' I added.

" 'It's the same thing,' Lu said, 'friendship is a ridiculous servitude. That idiot Ug is cultivating his good nature. He feels obliged to serve because I have let him accompany me for part of the way. We have spent the money he robbed under my strict supervision. I have taught him aspects of life that he could not have dreamed of, granting his evident and imbecilic breadwinner attitude, and now he starts with his touching gestures of sweaty sacrifice. Sweat repulses me. I can't stand it. The money you would bring would be stained with sweat, dripping thinks. No thanks, Ug! In this place I will give as long as I have. While I have, because I don't anymore and I'm getting out of here.'

"Obviously," Q continued, "Ug felt alluded to and timidly made this observation:

" 'It's not bad to serve. I like to serve, to be useful, going, coming, and doing things I'm told to do or that I think of.' (Here he smiled, waiting for a mocking comment, which nobody made.) 'I don't think there's anything wrong in serving or being a friend. Someone has to do things, love people and all that, while others say very important things and worry about reading, writing, making music, painting, discussing, and all that, which I can't express.' " (It was evident Don Q was trying to speak like a good man, but foolish.)

" 'Don't start bawling,' Lu told him forcefully.

" 'I'm surprised at you, Lu!,' Ug complained. 'Don't offend me!'

" 'He's not offending you,' I observed." (Don Q is speaking). " 'That's the way his pride allows him to thank you for your loyalty.'

" 'What pride? What thanks?' Lu interrupted me. 'You go around with your phrases and psychological profundities analyzing others as if we had asked you for it or as if you had the right to judge us: "you are this, you are that; and this is like this, and for this or for that, or for that over there . . ." I'm not investigating why you're playing the role of psychologist of souls—even the universal soul—although if I had time, and just to bother you, I would start thinking why you do and say things and why you feel like an important character. In one way or another you're converting me into some kind of Lucifer while you . . .'

" 'Oh!' interrupted thin Albert, who by now was half recovering from the slap and had regained his speech and even pardoned Ug. 'Oh! The great Q is the Guardian Angel of Paradise, always with his flaming sword in his hand, telling who is inside, who is outside, and why!'

" 'Wonderful! You finally said something intelligent, Von Albert,' Lu confirmed. 'It's true, Q is the Guardian Angel of chests and reserves that, I am sure, he believes to be filled with the secrets of the universe, always looking for someone to cut the apples so that he can pick up the cores and throw them beyond the limits of Paradise. Except that you don't need a sword for this, but a broom. Hail, great Broom Angel!' he said as he bowed to me.

"It was evident that the scene delighted Ug. He looked as

if he wanted to say, 'What a good point Lu made, the things he feels like saying!' "

("Heavens, Don Q!" I interrupted him. "Don Lu really thwarted you! I have always respected you for your solemnity; now I must add my admiration for your honesty in telling me these things. I thank you for it because now you have proven to be humble.")

"Well," he answered, "it was always like that with Don Lu; as soon as we saw each other we went at it. But then the important thing was to heat up the conversation in order to revive him. Now he wasn't answering me with merely a puff! There were words, cruelty, slaps, injuries, smiles: in other words, life circulated, although my vanity suffered a bit when other eyes saw me in such a light and I was judged by other intentions, and not by myself as was customary. But at that time, it was easy to get to the bottom of things and to ponder with all seriousness the problems of his suicide. That's how I had the opportunity to debate Don Lu. He was disturbingly young then and felt obliged to be enraged, because he didn't want to accept the simple life nor its fundamental faculties."

"Heavens, Don Q!" I answered him, "that explanation is a bit disillusioning. You were talking about very radical things, and suddenly your Lordship talks about youth and fear, placing a very transcendental polemic into a small psycho-historic framework, with which you acquire an undue advantage over Don Lu—who is not here to answer you unpleasantly—as well as over me because you have not given me material to infer by myself and from Don Lu how it really was. Thus you deprive me of the satisfaction of drawing my own conclusions and you monopolize the tale. But you have done it already. Go ahead! We were saying that you were the revered and great Broom Angel."

Don Q was a bit fretful over this, but, being honest, he made a slight "you are right" gesture and continued as follows:

"I had to become defensive, for I could do nothing but think about the broom, which distracted my attention for a while. Except that I didn't think of the broom as an instrument for sweeping but rather for flying, and I associated it with the Goya engraving in which there's a pestilent witch teaching a beautiful witch—who has her hands on the other one's shoulders, her face covered, and is sitting on the broom stick—how to fly it. This distracted me sufficiently so that Albert could observe:

" 'Perfect! You've got it. A strong sweep of the solemn knowledge of Don Q, who remains silent.'

"Pride, brooms, knowledge, silence! I had to summarize to regain my lead. Human relationship is so rich and suggestive! They force me to worry about myself as well as to justify myself. 'Really,' I added, 'I don't judge them. I only try to understand them, possibly so that I can understand myself. I don't know what's more touching, Ug's humility or Lu's efforts to maintain the line he chose, which has dragged him from young lord to possible suicide, skipping over Ug's thanks, Albert's expectation, and my own fear. I confess with all honesty that I fear your suicide as much as my own death. I fear it as a definitive demonstration, because there won't be room for corrections. There's only one opportunity, a credible one at least, to live, and it's the one we now confront, "right now," as we Mexicans say in our exquisite eagerness to make the present precise. I often think with much curiosity, and you should also, Don Lu, on the precise moment of witnessing our own death: the "right now" of our death, that irreducible, unmeasurable fraction, as indivisible as ourselves, that separates being and not-being, or, at least, being from not-knowing. Because I believe the way to be one's self is, basically, to know it. To be and to know, are . . .'

"Lu interrupted me:

CHAPTER XVII: *Reflections on Mexican Exquisiteness. The Innocent Blasphemy of a Cross-Eyed Jehovah, His Elbows on the Clouds, and the Beginning of the Interesting Theme of "Don Nobody, the One with Everyone's Faults," and Other Subtleties.*

" 'GO on with your Mexican exquisiteness, your spurts of wisdom, and your eternal suppositions. As always, we're talking, talking, categorizing, and making everything important. My problem is life not death, not life in general but my life, my own, the one I can't live as I want. Everything else you say doesn't matter to me.'

" 'But it does to me; I care very much about everything else. Something you say attracts my attention and I have theorized about it at great length: that you are travelling the road of death because you can't live as you want. How odd that something as vital as want can convert into death! That something originating in life can destroy it! Want against life! There is a monstrous error that someone has to be responsible for!'

" 'Don't be so dramatic, Don Q. You're giving life an importance it doesn't have. Nobody can be responsible for this filth. For whom and from what can there be responsibility? I imagine a cross-eyed Jehovah, elbows on the clouds, holding Ug accountable for robbing my father's coin collection (which nobody could use, full of dust and rot, which—converted to this century's money—was deliciously useful). Ug would tell Jehovah: "Lu is to blame, he persuaded me, showed me the way, forced me with moral pressures, told me where to sell them and how much to charge, etc., etc." ' ("I must report," Don Q clarified, "that here the poor Ug turned red and squirmed in his chair. He was going to speak, but Lu shut him up with a single gesture.")

" 'I, naturally, would recognize as truth whatever Ug might have said or screamed that was comprehensible. I would have told him, "Everything you say is true, but I have no one to answer to for whatever I felt like doing. The guilty one in this infernal confusion, if it's necessary to find him, is you. One eye would have blamed the other and this explains why he became cross-eyed. Responsibility would have been a ridiculous echo." '

" 'Don't be ridiculous!' Ug finally decided to speak. 'Don't be disrespectful. You're going to hurt yourself. Don't say those things! Don't be like that! Besides, I wouldn't blame you for anything. God knows why I did it. I . . .'

" 'Don't worry, my good Ug. There aren't nor can there be, judges. If there were judges, there would have to be judges for judges and the ultimate one of these would have to be cross-eyed. It's people like the solemn Don Q who are bent on that ridiculous question of responsibilities, which is a never-ending tale. They use responsibilities as a base to load whatever faults they choose onto the asses who want to carry them. Since I recognize neither judge nor ass, I don't admit any responsibility, nor do I blame anyone for anything!' "

("Listen Don Q," I interrupted, "What an odd expression!: 'blame anyone for anything . . .' "

"Yes," Don Q told me, "there's a subtle logic, well observed, especially by Spanish authors, with the only difference that for them no one is a 'don,' like me, due to the necessity of not personalizing anyone so as to blame him for the world's nothingness, which by the dialectical principle of the 'negation of negation' becomes the extraordinary affirmation that Nobody is guilty of everything, which is really what Don Lu was trying to say, so as to free God from responsibility, I think. In this respect Don Lu resembled all the great blasphemers, from Lucifer and Judas on." There's huge quarry to explore but he continued . . . "if it's all right with you.")

" 'It's not a problem of guilt but of responsibility,' I was forced to say, 'which is not the same if you study it carefully.'

" 'Q is getting subtle,' Albert announced.

" 'Just precise, because it's necessary to distinguish between being guilty and being responsible. The first idea is linked to the idea of sin and crime; the second, only to the basic idea of liberty, which is what brings people to dignity. On the other hand, it's the fountain of merit that is guilt's other extreme. Only a dignified person can be guilty or meritorious. Liberty acts between these two extremes.'

" 'The young master is discoursing,' Albert observed.

" 'Actually, he vomits his wisdom,' Lu emphasized, 'but for me there is a serious objection: he is guilty of his merit.'

" 'Another sweep,' Albert said, smiling.

"Ug didn't understand very well, but he smiled with relief, seeing that Lu was sputtering as he did when he was at his best.

" 'Precisely!' I confirmed. 'That's liberty's secret as well as the beautiful synthesis that, together with laughter, completes human dignity: to have the merit of guilt that is attained once it is recognized.'

" 'Well,' Lu said with a tone of compromise, 'tell me what you want me to recognize; what sins do you want me to repent now and at the hour of my death amen? Just leave me alone.'

" 'I don't want you to repent anything, because you're not guilty of your life. I only think you're responsible for your death. There are so many things to die for, that to die for nothing seems to me to be the greatest idiocy. I find no merit in it. It's the same to die for one thing or another. Death is death whatever its cause might be. If you're going to choose the hour of your death, you might as well choose the cause of it.'

" 'Heavens, Don Q . . . !' Lu began to interrupt, but Ug cut him off:

" 'Please, Lu, let him speak. I understand very well what he's saying and I have wanted to tell you so many times: let's die for something that is worth the effort and we will die together. In a fire saving children. Avoiding accidents. In a hospital giving blood. Let's even go to war!, or, or . . .' (It was evident that Ug's imagination had drained and was not going to give more of itself.)

" 'Of course,' I encouraged him, 'death is the same whether caused by sickness or by having your head split in a robbery, or by throwing yourself off a cliff so that the enemy may not take your flag. All have died. All of us will die. Nevertheless, there are deaths with merit and deaths that are just deaths. Because one has to choose, choose the cause of one's death. Because either you have your death's merit or you're guilty for your death, or . . .'

" 'Or you simply die,' Albert commented, 'which, on the

other hand, is what happens every day. Right now, I assure you there are many who are tranquilly dying. Just dying. Thinking about it, I don't know why we are showing so much fear!'

" 'What do you mean we are showing great fear!' Ug confronted him. 'Q is right. To me, although I'm very stupid, it can't escape me that, although no one asked for my consent to be born, I can choose, if there's an opportunity, the cause of my death. Gee! There's no reason why Lu should kill himself.' "

CHAPTER XVIII: *Wherein Don Lu's Presumed Sanctity Is Discussed and Immediately Retracted by His Satanic Pride Until It Is Almost Identified with Don Nobody Who Wanted to Die for Everything. Naturally the Brothers Karamazov Appear.*

" 'AH!' Lu laughed, 'You praise me, my dear gentlemen! You recognize the hero or martyr in me. Thank you! Already I can imagine a beautiful marble mausoleum on which the good Ug is sculpting with his huge hands whatever Q doctorally dictates while Albert, next to a cypress in the cemetery, and drunk, is shoving a can of beer down his throat in honor of my death: "Here lies Don Lu, vigorous defender of the people, who died for the fatherland wrapped in the heroically defended labarum . . ." Or: "Here, with the smell of sanctity but without his body rotting, lies Saint Lu, who died to redeem the sins of drunkards who frequented the tavern he used to patronize . . . !" No, my happy companions! Nothing like that, neither hero nor martyr. This conversation with the persuasive Don Q, something which I can't deny, has forced me to deeply analyze my situation and I have arrived at the conclusion that I really don't have motives that deserve, if we're talking about death, my death. If I'm really going to kill myself, I will do it for Nothing: I don't think I could do it for something.'

"We were getting to the bottom of things," (Don Q continued,) "and to close this open seam, I said:

" 'You see, my good Lu, how tremendously satanic your pride is? Are you so godly that you only accept Nothing as the motive of your death? Is there something worth living for? Is there something worth dying for?'

" 'Well, my dear Socrates,' Lu answered me, 'if you would like to know my most intimate thought, so that you may later dissect it in your lab, I will tell you: Why live if I can't find my leisure? My divine leisure! Climate and substance of my liking, my whatever-I-feel-like. Just like that: Whatever! Not compromised, nor bought, nor rented, nor sweated. Whatever I feel like. That's why I live. You find the formula—I won't—to how to live in unfathomable leisure, and I will readily continue living. But that possibility will arrive with no effort on my part. Just because I am what I am. That's the condition I impose on life, or I die. But I will not die of hunger, it would undoubtedly be unpleasant and the worst of possible tastes. It's better to bleed. What do you think? The last effort I made, just to find out my capacity for resistance, was that affair with the old man's coins, which you already know. But it was an excessive effort for my nerves. Too many uncontrolled emotions; too many instructions to that imbecile Ug who is full of childish scruples. I had to spend a night breaking his shell of honesty so that he would decide to do it, and he decided only when I got him drunk. And you know how he is when drunk. Well! I'm too lazy to tell you the last of my efforts to continue in leisure. Is it clear? In regard to my death, I tell you that, no, there's nothing worth dying for, except for nothing.' "

("Listen, Don Q, your tale is getting interesting. What an extreme posture this extraordinary Don Lu is assuming. Now I understand why you respect him and call him 'don'!")

"Yes," Don Q answered me, "he was a good 'don,' he was the closest thing I have found to the Don Nobody, who wanted to die for nothing, about whom we have spoken before.

"I suppose that some time he could have died for everything or for something, but he lacked vocation."

"This is really interesting," I had to insist. "He sounds like a character of a Russian novel of the last century. Don't you think so?"

"That might be because you want to be so vulgar and associate this autonomous tale to others: but if you wish to treat the theme I have no objection. If you notice, he was a kind of more radical Karamazov. He even had two brothers, deeply devoted to the feeling of tragic existence, something which they discovered at an early age. One died of delirium tremens because he was so weak; I think the other was killed by order of his wife. But that's another tale, two tales, which if you like I will tell you if I feel like it and if I'm in the mood. I think we should go on with this affair." Thus he continued:

CHAPTER XIX: *On Hegel, Mexicans, and Other Matters Which Are Treated Because "Time Is Ours; the Hour Is Holy and the Occasion Propitious for Such Chats."*

"TAKING advantage of something that I have just told you and that I anticipated by the urgency of your observations, I answered Don Lu:

" 'If you pay attention and you want to be sincere with yourself . . .'

" 'Oh, the wise advice of Polonius!' Albert interrupted.

" '. . . with yourself, because you have no reason why you should be sincere with us, or with me, for to die for nothing is to die for everything . . .'

" 'You are becoming paradoxical, my good Sancho,' Lu interrupted me. 'Unamuno is already riding around on a silver stallion.'

" 'He hasn't had dinner,' Albert explained. 'I got him out of his room early and look what time it is.' (It was after eleven at night.)

" 'The only thing I can offer you,' Ug said obligingly, 'is a bit of corn-flour porridge, really thick, which the cook made before she left because we didn't pay her. That Unamuno must be a peasant because the name sounds Basque.'

"I paid no attention to the interruption and continued:

" '. . . to die for nothing is to die for everything. Look, Lu, I believe that deep inside you are a redeemer: you want to redeem the world's leisure because you found the world redeemed from sins. I must recognize that it is good to go deep into the theme because many problems that concern me are at stake: freedom of will, which is a passionate theme; the Absolute Spirit after Hegel's and the Mexican heritage that few understand and that you share in an unconscious form, my dear Lu, and that which I call "the firm will of leisure," which is celebrated "right now," and is put off until tomorrow and Saint Monday are sanctified. If you will allow me, and considering that it's not yet twelve, a magical hour set by Lu to leave this life, due to some absurd Cinderella complex, I could develop that theme, because time is ours, the occasion propitious and . . .'

" 'No, not Hegel, no, please!' Albert requested.

" 'No, "Mexican curios," no!' Lu protested.

"Ug said nothing, he just laughed, relieved."

("Listen, Don Q," I interrupted him, "how could you seriously propose a question like that at such a peculiar moment? It's natural that this motley group wouldn't have admitted it; I would have seriously suspected that you were adorning the tale because such an academic threat in no way fits the logic of the events, nor the psychology of the protagonists such as their idiosyncrasies were. It's impossible to even assume that, at a quarter to twelve, someone, even you, could be involved in these conversations . . .")

"I was simply trying to overcome you with a transcendental conversation, to break up the purpose," Don Q answered me with some ingenuity, "but it didn't catch on."

"Well," I told him, "the fact that you mention the theme indicates to me that you want to develop it, and being that between you and me 'time is ours; the hour holy and the occasion propitious for such chats,' well, let's go ahead!"

(My great daring can't be denied, not only for not admitting, but rather for somehow provoking, a new interruption, when the tale had already become a dialogue of relative agility; at least sufficiently loose and even somewhat tasty. But being that we are not trying to find out what happened with the already-presented suicide affair, and with the porridge already mentioned—to my relief, because I didn't know how the famous remedy was going to arrive—but rather to narrate for posterity Don Q's affairs, I resolved to invite him to develop a theme that evidently interested him. It would have seemed extremely unjust to me that—besides Lu, Albert, and Ug—I should also refuse to know what those semitragic, albeit happy companions, had determinedly refused to let be said. It's not impossible that this is the only opportunity for me to say what is probably going to be said, because, although I must warn you that Don Q almost told it to me then, if I don't tell it now, I may simply forget it, and it would then remain in the enormous and unfathomable store of things that have been thought but have not been said, and in which probably could be found, registered in some form of memory, the best of things, those things that quiet people have thought of; those who don't have the vanity to think they have something to say; the lonely ones who had no one to tell them to; the desperate ones who didn't have the chance to say it; the humble who have not given themselves the importance to bother with it; the egotists who have not wanted to convey them, and all the others we can imagine who had something to say but never said it. I find it sad that Don Q's questions could even be found in that situation, because someone might be interested in this strange mixture between one of Don Q's grandfathers, Don William Frederick Hegel, and the Mexicans. Because some of you probably don't want to follow me, as an alternative I propose you skip to the corresponding page where you will find the continuation of a tale that has extended far beyond what I planned, so much so that it resembles the tale of the good pipe.)

CHAPTER XX: *Wherein Is Opened a Parenthesis to Treat Some Quetzalcoic Questions and Wherein Redemption, Sin, Guilt, the Exile of Chaos, Transcendent Humility, and Other Equally Important Mexican Matters Are Discussed.*

FINALLY, I proposed to Don Q that he open a parenthesis, and, after some reticence, he opened it to tell me what follows:

"Well then, my intrigued and good Don Josefo" (you must remember that he called me 'don' whenever I earned the right to be called that, either by my questions, intelligence, or by the felicity of my observation). "I have always thought that we Mexicans, like an echo of self-sacrifice we accept from Quetzalcoatl, preserve an invincible eagerness to denigrate ourselves, to wound ourselves and to bleed through self-inflicted wounds in an effort to save our world from ridicule or the other world's disdain, conscious that one and the other, laughter and disdain, correspond to the heap of the most intimate of human essences, those which fit directly into dignity. I will speak to you some other time about this, if you'd like; for now, accept it. Well then, in that effort to wound ourselves we recognize we have all the defects of men, in the same way that pre-revolutionary Russians felt responsible for all the sins of humanity. I think that in each case there is a decided Messianism that is or is not deserved (I fear ridicule, I assert it categorically), but that in any case conditions our conduct. And it couldn't be any other way (and here I will extend myself, be patient with me). Remember that our aboriginal peoples recognized as their responsibility—pay attention: responsibility, not guilt, so that you can understand well my conversation with Don Lu—the keeping of heavenly luminaries in their sockets and orbits. They closely attended to that responsibility: either with self-sacrifice, pain, and blood spilled not to redeem sins, it's true, but to nourish the heavens, which is one of the Quetzalcoic sentiments, or with a stranger's blood, spilled for the same cosmic end, which was the Tezcatlipoic sentiment of which Huitzilopochtli was a significant expression."

(I open a parenthesis. Although it was evident to me that Don Q didn't know Nahuatl, it was clear that he liked the words of a language which had the good judgment to eliminate the sounds of "r" and double "r," horrendous sounds, as he used to tell me.)

". . . In our Indian world there wasn't, appropriately, the idea of sin, a transcendent fault; but there was, and this is important, an incredible sense of man's responsibility to creation, which we have to understand in order to understand ourselves. In his modesty, the Indian never believed himself the object of creation. He only recognized, with firm humility, his responsibility to keep it, to serve it expecting no reward, outside of the consciousness of sharing and living in it. Our people did not sin; they simply became responsible, which is a dignified, humble, moving, and disturbing way to react before the mystery we want to sift with our science or our will until we arrive at an incomprehensible buzz that makes saints of a few, others wise, and many others nothing more than blasphemers. Well then, Indian man was not a man of guilt and sin but of responsibilities. In his humility he did not construct a paradise or even a hell for man: he only conceived of the anonymous glory of maintaining creation, of letting blood, one's own and that of strangers, in the furious effort to love their gods who fed not on human conduct but rather on man's pain. It was not conduct which praised the gods, it was the pain for which our old people became responsible, a pain which, notice well, was not a punishment but a fluke of contribution. It didn't matter how one lived, but how and why one died. Notice how different . . ."

"Listen, Don Q. All this is very interesting, but I don't find it related to what you were telling me. It might be that I'm very objective and I don't understand these primitive brutalities which you deal with so subtly."

Don Q answered me quite seriously:

"Be patient, Pepe, these are important things, things about which we let the rest speak and which we never stop except to destroy them. Wait a bit, later on I will speak about other things that are more comprehensible to you."

"Forgive me, Don Q, but now, as always, we start with the 'now' and the 'here' of a flower, as Hegel used to say, and we will never know where and how we are going to pick up the fruit."

"Wait, let me tell it to you from the beginning, to explain to you how our self-destructive effort has confused our transcendent humility with 'feelings of inferiority,' and our consciousness of the present with 'irresponsibility,' which is the connecting theme which brought us, by your asking, you have to admit it, to this conversation. Let me continue." And he continued as follows:

"It's important to be aware that our Indian man was not one who loved, but one who hurt. He was not born to love, but to pain. In one or another way you have to recognize that, in the branches of the cross, in one you find love and in the other pain, expressed in the sacrifice's mystery, familiar or foreign, voluntary or imposed; but in any case, suffering. Our people deeply lived the tenderness of pain and accepted it in all its transcendence and took it to its final conclusion with a deeper responsibility than that of any other people, though all peoples, in some moment of confrontation with the mystery, have resorted to sacrifice to resolve or to favor it. I, I must tell you, deeply love my Indian essence, its primogenial responsibility deeply moves me, accepted with the deepest humility that any race has imposed on itself. I love my roots, Pepe, these and the others that cross the sea, one side going to the Pyrenees the other to Africa. I love Indians, my own, in their deep horror of chaos, in their painful cosmic responsibility, in their incredible devotion to the order of creation; although these days they can't do anything but join us to make a great union, with all the defects and virtues, and to convey to us their deep tenderness towards the world, their order, and pains."

"Just a moment, Don Q, one moment. Why this sudden declaration? I'm not asking you for anything! It seems you're justifying yourself. I only try, nothing more, to arrange this conversation so that it may be fruitful. Suddenly you come at me with unbound passion . . ."

"Yes, a great passion for my things, for my roots, for those roots that link me to the world, stuck to its roundness, the same ones that allow me to understand the human race, to love and to suffer it, the deeper the better.

"I love my people, which is a way of loving Humanity. I would like to suffer for them."

"Come on, Don Q! You too are turning into a redeemer! Calm down! Think about what you're saying. How is your suffering going to help your people? It's sterile, irrational, senseless. You're always analyzing, so serenely, so solemn, and suddenly you break the dams of reason and want to resolve problems with pain and suffering. I can just see you licking cactus flowers with your tongue and making your lips bleed! Don't be crass, Don Q! What's wrong with you? Calm yourself! Calm yourself!" (I must say that Don Q's fits were not frequent. Nevertheless, at that time, surely stimulated by the suicide tale, he was particularly effusive and disoriented in his conversation and judgments. You are probably noticing this.)

CHAPTER XXI: *Concerning Pain and How It Works, with Complementary Reflections on Faith in the World's Just Harmony, the Value of Resignation and Fundamental Attitudes Towards the Being, plus More Transcendental Exquisiteness.*

"LET me tell you this or I'll explode," Don Q continued. "I have it here" (he hit his chest) "and I haven't been able to articulate it. Listen to me: You know what happens with work and why it works? We lack the technique to do good or to solve questions. You give yourself up to pain due to the desperation of ignorance before the force of your own good will. You want but you are not able to. You don't understand that it is not enough to want, and then desperation makes you give over to pain. That's why primitive people suffer. There's either pain or technique. To want is what's important. It is, notice, a problem of the efficiency of conduct. When conduct reaches its limit, the will's force overflows and takes the mysterious path of pain and sacrifice, searching for the compensation that practice does not attain. It sees in pain's will the most profound human protest against feebleness. It doesn't have the strength to do it; but you can give your pain to overcome, or at least compensate for impotence. Of course there's irrationality (reason is so new to the world); of course there's ignorance, which is a form of impotence. Now explain to yourself that, due to a lack of capacity, there are moments in which I want to surrender to pain. I have seen so many of our people suffer so many times! But not with that pain that is accepted by the order of things. That seems to be an evil, stupid pain which also makes me suffer. I'm talking about searched pain, about accepted pain, embraced pain. It's the money with which the poor, the wretched, or the humble pay God."

"Listen to me, Don Q, I wish Don Lu were here so that he could respond to you with something that is tickling me and that I would like to tell you about . . ."

"Don't tell me. Just shut up. I know what you would say and of course I can answer you: I don't know what good is man's pain to God; I don't know what role it plays in the universe. The only thing I want to emphasize is that existing (when you accept it, you pay) redeems debts or buys promises to the extent to which your will is oriented towards it. It's with the last coin that you buy or pay for definite things. There is a horrible resemblance between pain and death: one suffers and dies in a thousand ways; but there are forms of suffering and dying attached to the sacrificial vocation, and then merit results, deserving, which is really faith in the form of justice, the deep conviction that in some way love will have its balance. Be warned that, profoundly, the people that suffer are affirming their faith in the universe's harmony and equilibrium. Our Indian world put all its pain on one side of the scale so that the universal equilibrium could be maintained. That's why I admire those who suffer and resign themselves. Therefore, as well you know, I love Beethoven."

(I can do nothing less than observe Don Q's picturesque fits. Notice what his themes of reflection were. Possibly he was not wrong! It's true that rude and ignorant people make sacrifices instead of using antibiotics: they walk on their knees to obtain a good harvest because they don't have a good tractor or fertilizers. I believe that technique, with all that it supposes, is an enormous apparatus through which knowledge is redeeming its pain. I would have liked to talk about this question with Don Q. But it wasn't the type of thing that attracted him! There's no mystery in technique. But it interests me deeply, although I'm a simple, modest man of letters. The difference between my civilized objectivity and Don Q's primitive subjectivity, will undoubtedly protect me from criticism, as I have carefully intended. I will continue that singular character's tale.)

"Don't believe," he added, "that this, which I passionately tell you, is madness, nor that I have lost sight of this parenthesis' purpose. It's only that one thing carries another, each moment its flower and each flower its fruit at the same moment. But our Indian universe moves me, I owe so much to it, although I think like a Westerner. I believe only a few people have had a humility as deep as ours. Humility is not a feeling of inferiority but rather a severe sense of universal proportion and a full consciousness of mystery. I'm not going to praise humility. It already has been done by Christian authors and saints and contradicted by the madness of proud Christians. Reading the Chilam Balam I found this question, of such anguishing humility that, by itself, it sanctifies the Indian world:

" 'Am I someone?' man says in his spirit.

" 'Am I the one I am?' he says in the middle of the earth.

"These questions were a brutal test for my 'Ieity,' because I understood the most radical humility that any man has admitted before the universe.

"Concerning the problem of being, the great books have said extraordinary phrases:

" 'I am the one who is,' Jehovah says.

" 'I am who I am,' Quixote asserted.

" 'To be or not to be?' Hamlet proposed.

"But no one, from the deepest part of his I, and before the spasm of the infinite, has asked himself if it is someone and if he is what he is. His doubt is even more radical in his unfinished humility than that observation which results from 'life is a dream, and dreams themselves are only dreams.' Note well, bachelor of law, note well: there is someone who has asked himself if he is someone; there is someone who has asked himself if he is the one he is. Don't you find it extraordinary, of an incredible depth? Don't you think it is one of the most serious questions that have been proposed for anxiety against the I's existence and persistence? Notice the profundity of the question: it is not now a matter of knowing what or who I am; it's only asking if he's someone, if he is the one he is, which is worth the same as inquiring what role this is that I am playing in the inscrutable problem of universal conscience. Don't you think?"

I took advantage of this last question to make an observation on this point, risking, of course, incurring Don Q's disgust; but because the conversation had taken such weird turns, I thought it lost nothing if it was interrupted, because I was really tired of going from flower to fruit and from fruit to flower. I told him:

"Listen, Don Q, you always give too many transcendental meanings to things, even the simplest ones. If you ask me what I think of that question to which you give so much significance and sense, I have to tell you that to me it seems a terribly naive primitivism, senseless. It is contradictory and stammering. Finally, I don't know why you bother with these things and draw inferences, conclusions, get excited, even become exalted. Analyze the question reasonably and you will agree with me that inquiry is meaningless. Finally, as to what you are asking: I invite you to analyze piece by piece and you will see how . . ."

I couldn't finish. Don Q fixed his eyes on me until I had to lower my own. He made me nervous and told me:

"See why I call you the bachelor Pepe Seco? Because your soul is dissected into three or four branches of analysis, or five, ten, or whatever you want to analyze what I tell you. There are words that are not words; questions that are not questions: they are stars, and the ones I told you are that: stars, spheres, and music. If you have, and you do, a dry soul and feeble imagination, they mean nothing to you. I'm sorry for you. Resign yourself to your imbecilic nationality. Cut your wings and stuff your breast, dry your heart and fill your big head with the sawdust of analysis, that stuff that remains after you shake Porfirio's tree. If you don't understand the importance of the affair I'm talking about, I had better shut up and forget the whole matter."

He remained silent without taking his eyes off me. A tense situation was created because I couldn't remain with my eyes lowered, and I knew that, if I met his eyes, we were going to fight and I didn't want to go to that extreme. So, with the best of my smiles I was able to tell him despite my stammering:

"Don Q, don't be intolerant! I'm very interested in what you say and think, precisely because I myself can't think it or say it. But to me it seems flagrantly unjust that you get annoyed because I sincerely think and speak the things that your conversation suggests to me. It's not fair! I beg you to go on! Forgive me, don't get impatient and tell me I can't express my opinion and must simply listen. I want to keep the privilege of your friendship and it would be very painful for me if you were to be annoyed and deprive me of your conversation. I recognize my faults. Actually I have dried up as time has passed and I have imposed demands on myself. I have compromised, I admit it. With all humility I beg you to tell me if, in my disagreeable dryness, you consider me someone, and if you do so, to please go on."

Don Q smiled at my interruption and said:

"Of course you are someone: you are a dry, analytic bachelor whom, despite all, I appreciate and with whom I like to converse, for otherwise I would be delivering monologues, which besides being rather monotonous is extremely sterile. Well, let's forget this incident and go ahead with the question."

(He continued as follows, but it's clear that I remained firm in my impression that Don Q was an unusually fantastic being who could draw transcendental inferences from anything that impressed him, and that he frequently created absurd and unexpected situations. But that was precisely what made him picturesque, and why I bother with him.)

"I was telling you all that," Don Q continued, "to accredit the peculiar condition of our Indian world, in which you are involved in some way, even though you're not aware of it. I wanted to accredit a fundamental thing, on which I must insist, although I see in your eyes the vacuum of incomprehension and even some expression of jest. But I don't care. I already forgave you and in so doing I justify the possibility of continuing to speak to you about what interests me. Look, I want to point out that while the Indian was autonomous and depended on himself, he cultivated the responsibility of keeping universal order by the cult of blood and pain. Note well so that you don't classify it as transcendental masochism as some imbeciles have done. Pain as part of a cult, not as a punishment but as the human being's most exquisite obligation, of a higher category than morality itself. They raised to a maximum norm something that in some way beats in all of the world's religions: sacrifice. But none reached the bottom, like ours, which, as I have told you, kept it close to this shore.

"Regarding that idea, or better, for that purified responsibility, for that cosmic jealousy, they built an order and maintained an incredible discipline. Pay attention, Josefo, an incredible discipline, of an inflexible rigidity, especially expressed in that eponymous people, the Aztecs. Remember how they lived and died by iron and blood: their gods became demons, their kings slaves and their vassals dust. The world emptied of its responsibilities. What was it given in return? You're going to tell me the other side of the cross. The love doctrine (imposed by blood, of course); but, note well, they were offered a whole doctrine of conduct to obtain personal salvation. Something that had never occurred to them. Another world, Josefo! Another world! An egotistical world, if you study it well: a good business, exchanging conduct and good intention for an eternity of prosperity. Another world! How different from the stifled sacrifice without personal hope! To go from giving everything to asking for everything. A total upturning: no transcendental responsibility for the species; only the expectation of glory and of personal immortality. A small thing for those who carry on their shoulders the responsibility of creation by means of anonymous sacrifice. Do you see, my esteemed Josefo?" (Here Don Q, by way of inquiry, fixed huge eyes on me.) "Do you see how suddenly a whole race is left without responsibility? Notice: harsh, brutal, the Indian universe sunk in the Glory of the Western Lord and a whole race remained without mission, without responsibility, with all its pain but without feeling or hope. Its pain became the sordid misery of that one who has no other transcendent object than saving himself. What a contrast!: from saving the universe, from feeding the sun so that it would have strength and be able to overcome the dead of Mictlan, which hang on to it in their effort to make the cosmos' order right, to continue suffering to save themselves."

CHAPTER XXII: *Wherein Continue Don Q's Reflections on the Indian World and Its Capacity for Renunciation to Save the World. Don Q Utters a Chilling Prophecy.*

WHEN he got to this point, I could not but interrupt Don Q, who, in my opinion, was going too far. I implored him:

"Listen, Don Q. Are you aware that you're justifying human scarifices, the shedding of one's own and someone else's blood on the altars of idols for primitive and absurd beliefs? How can you possibly be involved in such misleading considerations that lack all sense and logic? With good reason did Western man raze that absurd world and replace it with the doctrine of loving your fellowman. Are you a heathen or what? Why have you tried to terrify me? Just a while ago you didn't want Lu to commit suicide, and now you're justifying human sacrifice and idolatrous aberrations. Who can understand you? Not I!"

"Don't be retarded, my little Pepe! Don't be retarded! You're forcing me to resort to children's explanations. If anyone believes in the universal function of egotism, it is I, involved as you know with my Ieity and desperately disposed to save myself. I was simply (it's a shame I have to explain it) describing that world and comparing it with another, in its ultimate consequences, its quintessences. Forget about idols and anecdotes. Put aside the stone of sacrifices and the damsels thrown to the underground pools. Forget about blood and keep your attitudes. I never imagined that you, in your regretful lack of imagination, would convert to idolatry and begin sacrificing people or bleeding yourself. We know the worlds keep their orbits through complicated laws of celestial mechanics, in which it is sure that pain accounts for nothing. It is obvious that the Indian allowing himself to be sacrificed had no effect on the sun. The only thing I ask is that you put yourself in his place and try to act as if it were true that the sun, to come out, requires sacrifice. Elevate to a maxim of observance the necessity of providing this sacrifice, and try to understand what an authentic cosmic responsibility it was, in which the individual fused himself while waiting for nothing less than the banishment of chaos. Analyze the principles and attitudes, not the scientific value of suppositions. Think. What would you do if one demanded your pain for the sun to come out?"

I confess I tried to understand it but couldn't. Nevertheless, I made a gesture of agreement, and Don Q continued his conversation:

"I want you to understand well what happens to a people when you suddenly take away the highest responsibility that any human race could ever have imposed on itself. Imagine the deafening silence in the Indian world when it turned out that not only did they not have the responsibility, they had not the right to personal salvation, because their sins had already been redeemed by the blood of a son who had an amorous, sweet, tender mother. A whole saga losing its content; a whole race deprived of mission, the mission its own genius and peculiar vocation had imposed on itself."

"But, Don Q," I interrupted him, "I still don't understand how it's possible that you, especially you, are somehow justifying the sadomasochism of sacrifice by means of absurd suppositions and with an aim towards irrational purposes. It's irritating to waste so much breath. What can happen to a people deprived of such a horrible vice? Nothing! They must have felt free from an absurd burden. Besides, Don Q, you talk about people, race, Indian man, as if they were permanent entities, but forgive me, generations which follow misguided generations don't even have to remember why, educated as they are in a totally different philosophy. I don't believe you have the right to draw conclusions about our contemporaries based on what occurred centuries ago. I can in no way admit what you say about 'the vacuum of responsibility for Indian man,' nor those things that you are surely going to say as a consequence of what you've told me."

"Look, my polemic bachelor: what you want is to discuss argumentatively, and that can't be done. I don't argue; I exhaust myself; things flow from me according to the stimuli I receive and according to a mass of imponderables that I refuse to analyze. Yet, it is convenient to clarify something elementary for your myopic vision. It is evident that the transcendental supposition of the Indian world was not certain. Of course, sacrifice and pain cannot be used to complete the sun's rotation and to banish chaos. That doesn't modify the situation. The error having been discovered, human sacrifice becomes sterile, an assassination, what you lawyers call crimes under the Penal Code. But only after the error was discovered and proven, not before; the consequence is worthy beforehand because the supposition is admitted. It's a problem of sincerity of purpose and faith in the process, or (so that you may understand it with your forensic language, 'admit without conceding and put yourself in the absurd hypothesis') that the order of things is as the Indian world said it was. Soak yourself with that supposition and you will see, if you're sincere and profound, how, as the world of Indian intentions gets larger the Western world gets smaller, because in its history, only One and perhaps a few others spilled their blood to save the moral world. The rest of us have been redeemed. All Indians were redeemers, of course, not of the moral world, for it must be said that they never asked that question; but they did ask about the cosmic world, the sun's beauty and the beauty of stars; they asked about order, which they rescued periodically from the horror of chaos and the terrible vacuum of nothingness." (This last matter was spoken by Don Q in a slow, whispering tone which, I confess, impressed me.) "That aptitude of race has not been substituted for any other mission: our people held the vessel of redemption as responsibility and not the licentious condition of redeemed sin. Someday" (here Don Q raised his voice and almost screamed) "in some way, the Indian blood that remains, mixed in the veins and arteries with the blood of more egotistical peoples, will contribute to generously redeem the world, asking in return nothing more than the glory of universal order. Someday, and that day will be the dawning of the human race. Someday there will be a mission, a responsibility that will rattle the generous extinct volcano of Indian renunciation. Hear it and tremble! It will be the end of the world of redeemed hypocrites, of proud inheritors of another's pain, of full stomachs, vain intentions, and hollow prides. It will be a new era. . . !"

Don Q remained silent for a while. I confess that I did not consider it opportune to break his silence, for it was evident that the man was exalted by his prophecy, which, I must also say, I felt as an indirect threat to my person and temperament. A few minutes having passed, Don Q continued as follows:

"I'm convinced that, the Indian's racial mission having ended, his world sank into silence and never again became interested in another responsibility. They accuse them, we accuse them of being sluggish, idle, irresponsible, taciturn, contemplative, aimless. What have we given them in return? Work in mines, quarries, unskilled jobs in businesses? What do vermin like you have to offer them? Incorporation into technical progress, the confusion of enterprise, urban proletarianization? What do you offer them? Penicillin and tractors? A small thing for an enormous interior world, terrifyingly empty."

"Now I protest!" I interrupted him. "What you're telling me is a variant on the literary and romantic attitude of dealing with the Indian world. Your position is inhibiting and sterile. Not content with threatening me with your ridiculous and improbable prophecies, you accuse me as if I were a commissioner, and you seem to find it commendable if in some way the sacrifices, bloody altars, and the horrors of the sordid, absurd, primitive world were to come back. You have become overheated by your lucubrations, and in your eagerness for transcendentalities you have lost the track and gone mad. I can't understand it, as much as . . ."

Don Q interrupted me in turn:

"You are more limited than I had imagined. You don't

understand anything. You will never understand the transcendence of principles and the importance of primogenial attitudes. I would get annoyed with you if I stayed here, so I end this conversation."

CHAPTER XXIII: *Wherein the Thread of the Tale of the Frustrated Suicide Is Picked Up Again. Reflections on Guilt and the Necessity of Pardon to Inaugurate Virgin Times.*

HE left disgusted, without speaking of Hegel or Mexicans or the absolute spirit or leisure. These items will probably remain in the store of things thought but never spoken. Later, however, and already calmed, he did express something. I had met him by accident and said:

"Listen, Don Q, you never finished telling me about that suicide and the host of tricks. We got stuck in a lamentable discussion about human sacrifices and you left me extremely depressed. I hope time has calmed you down. For my part, I must tell you that I have repented, and I hope you will forgive me if I said anything impertinent."

"Stop these idiocies, Pepe Seco. What you have just said about time and forgiveness is very important. So I forgive you, if I have to forgive you at all. I will continue the tale of Don Lu later. But at the moment I'm thinking about the enormous importance of guilt and sin in the moral world. Forgiveness is antimemory which, I remember I once told you, is antitime. If you understand dialectically what I have just told you, it turns out that forgiveness is the generating resource of the new opportunities for virgin times. In a moral world of faults without pardon, we would always be linked to the past. We would only be the history of our faults, without possible redemption. Forgiveness was another great invention. I forgive you, Josefo! I forgive you!"

"What a relief you provide me, Don Q, and not merely because it sheds a little light on the darkness in which our last conversation left us. Then you were speaking about blood and pain. Now, I confess, I feel a sort of caress with what you tell me about forgiveness. It's another world, although as ordinary. I don't understand those 'antis' you tell me about and least of all that odd thing about the 'virgin times.' "

"Of course, it's another world. That's the world of lights and jaguars. The world of pricks and hooks which are good for hurting and banishing the chaos. The one I'm telling you about is a different world. This is the world of human intimacy, the intimate world of the will that constructs its own interior harmony. You probably still think I'm crazy, as you told me last time. Try to understand me: I'm the type who tries to understand everything and who can barely contain himself. It has moved me, I want to be frank with you, that you have asked me for forgiveness, and it attracts my attention that almost simultaneously you have spoken about time. I'm going to put myself in the hypothesis of guilt, oldest daughter of freedom, and as I once told you, the carnal sister of merit."

(This barbarous Don Q used to say such important things, don't you think? I don't know where he discovered so many. It seems as if he were in a constant state of ebullition. I understood a few, many bored me and some gave me courage. But this one turned out rather amiable, so that, if you like, I will continue the conversation with Don Q.)

"Well then, the world of guilt is an exclusively human world and primitively interior. The moon's light doesn't reach it and there is no law of gravity in it. It is not a world of cognition but of recognition. You recognize your fault when you contemplate your intentions and your conduct with all your freedom. You are the judge of your guilt. Only you, exclusively you. Once recognized, it fixes itself with all the horror of History and it would be eternal if there were no pardons or punishment. But who forgives and why? Note well, little man, that you are dealing with judges of justice and punishment, with who forgives and why. You yourself? Of course not. You can repent, which is the price of recognition and your torture. You can punish yourself. But you can't forgive yourself. Who forgives then? Is it that man is horribly alone and there's no one who can forgive him? Tell me, you, man of laws, who forgives? Who forgives the guilty? I need God to forgive me! If he didn't exist, my need for pardon would have to invent him! Because it's that or pain again, only this time as punishment. It would again be the supposition that the world's harmony sadistically demands punishment for the remission of faults. Pain again? And what for? Does pain rise like copal, like incense to inebriate the gods? Are recognized faults purged merely with pain on the cosmic platform? There has to be a pardon, to be able to start anew, to inaugurate virgin times; to not lose oneself in the oppression of memory."

"Listen, Don Q, to hear you speak is like hearing a great sinner and I know that you're a fundamentally good man, that at least you don't act up. You only think and think. I'm ratifying my opinion that you're too mystical. You're more or less setting up problems like a church father, or a great Indian priest of long ago." (What I didn't tell him, and I think I was right not to, was that what he liked was to make phrases.)

"But," I told him, "I recall that Don Lu argued with you about the existence of fault itself. What if there isn't a transcendental fault? Why do you torture yourself with this question of punishment and pardon, which truly opens a soft spot in the world of possibilities? It's something like a father embracing his children; it's an amorous refuge where one is under the covers, safe from the cold of the universe."

"Of course," he told me, "as if one were submitted to one's own Ieity; it is, as I told you, a direct and exclusive relation of your conduct with yourself; it doesn't leave the realm of your individuality . . . except if the necessity of punishment or the possibility of pardon is considered, like forms of the autogeneration of the opportunity of becoming better, it's then that you feel the necessity of a punishing God or a forgiving God. The terrible God of judgments who makes Western man shake!

"But you have to understand that this is an accepted and recognized world: the world of guilt. Admit it and the rest will come by itself. Better yet: admit your freedom and you will find fault and merit, the two sides of conduct, which take you to punishment or glory . . . or to a horrendous silence: the intranscendence of your bound conduct, that is, to the I's definitive transitoriness; which is my anxiety of persistence's anguish; that anxiety I sometimes share with my uncle Miguel.* " He remained silent.

"What can I tell you, Don Q, if you can't penetrate this problem?"

* Later on I became aware that Don Q took the liberty of considering himself Unamuno's nephew.

CHAPTER XXIV: *On Free Will.*

"IF only I could explore!" he screamed, almost exalted. "If only I could explore! I'm the master of my will and I'm completely responsible for my own conduct. Many times I have thought that, together with the other centers of conduct to which I relate and which I might relate to, I am, as they are, like the free tip of a tape originating in the infinite and destined for the infinite, which has become tangled in the compass of elapsed times and joined spaces. I am responsible for my senses because I am, like all those who are, a top of the infinite that only faces a time emptied of everything, in which I'm knitting my own conduct. I don't know if later my conscience will shine contemplating these clots of my past actions, the good and the bad; but now, at this moment I conceive of freedom, my own, and I am free. Because of my freedom, I hold myself responsible for the elapsed times before whoever wants to make worthy the necessity or the fatality of my conduct. I am a peak of the infinite in search of new times! I even know I am free from the personal God who would have created me and whose forgiveness I would have to ask! I don't know if you understand."

He then painted for me—for he also painted—a picture in which there were strange-colored serpentines originating in circles and changing into figure eights that came together in the same serpentine in which there was a kind of projected face in what he called "the curdle of time," with hands pointing behind and ahead, and in both cases hands beating what could be the chest. A rare thing that I also did not understand, surely, although I didn't tell him because he supposed that I was clearing my stupor. I left him in doubt and told him:

"Odd painting, Don Q. What would you call it?"

" 'On Free Will,' " he answered very seriously and added, "Now you understand, don't you?"

"No, Don Q, frankly I didn't understand it, really . . . I don't think it's a painting because it's not self-explanatory; it's more like literature."

"It's true," he told me, "it's the closest thing to logistic expression—from Logos—from the liberty that one has tried to shape. You don't understand it. It may be that I don't either. But I don't think I have wasted my time. At least I have tried to express myself, and a song without a pentagram has left my painful soul: the Hymn of my liberty in the infinite."

He remained with an expression of great placidity on his thin face (because Don Q, naturally, was thin, although quite strong, and he was proud of his strength. Strange, don't you think?).

CHAPTER XXV: *Wherein the Suicide Affair Is Continued with Further Reflections on the Redemption of Leisure.*

I took advantage of the occasion to beg him to go on with the old tale of Don Lu's frustrated suicide, and, giving in, he told me:

"You remember that we were dealing with the affair of leisure's redemption, which contained Don Lu's attitude, and that they did not allow me to academize with Hegel, and I plunged with you into the labyrinths of the cosmic world of our Indian world?

"I must tell you that the rejection of a conversation theme alone, so energetically asserted by Don Lu, already revealed a decision to live, from which I gathered I was achieving my purpose, so I then told them:

" 'All right, I will not mention the topic if it bothers you.'

" 'It bothers us,' Albert and Don Lu said in unison. 'It definitely bothers us.'

" 'Well,' I added, 'at least my observation remains that with your death you're redeeming the world's leisure.'

" 'Jokes! Empty phrases,' Don Lu answered me. 'None of that! I don't redeem anything, nor do I pretend to do so with my death. I don't express any will with my death wish, other than disappearing from an absurd world whose order does not admit my will to exist. An idiotic world full of work in which work guarantees nothing; full of sickness, smelly puddles, absurd pain, and misery. A world full of injustices, prayers, superstitions, and absurd rites. A world full of slaps on the cheeks, a world full of routine and constructed without imagination. It would have been so easy for whoever might have done it to cover the earth's roundness with pure lilies of the field, a flower which I have on my family's coat of arms. So easy! But instead, nothing: dogs that piss on trees, fight over bitches, smell their behinds and then lick your hand with the same snout. One single snout in dogs and men. One single snout to kiss and blaspheme, to pray and vomit, a single duct to procreate and urinate. What a horrible lack of imagination! And everything else is just like it. What a horrendous world. I neither recognize it nor want it for myself! The more I speak with you, the more I convince myself that I want to leave. And for your information, whatever I do or don't find later is better than this idiotic filth. If there's nothing, fine! And if there is and I don't like it and they give me the freedom to leave, I will leave and I will go on committing suicide as long as I feel like it.'

" 'Ay, Chihuahua!' Albert said in a well-cultivated German accent, 'that's what he will call, undoubtedly, a firm perishing vocation . . .'

" 'Exactly!' Don Lu accepted. 'Exactly!: a firm, rooted, and well-measured will to perish; among other things so that insects like Albert will not censure you and gravely insult your person.'

" 'I realize', I added, 'that this is an imperfect world. All forms immersed in the infinite flow are. Only the will to want the perfect is perfect; but impotent. Deeply within your vocation for leisure, you are showing your will for perfection, which is really a way to love God.'

" 'What God?' Don Lu contradicted me. 'Why do you include that man in these things? Leave him alone, seated in his clouds and playing with the little toys he invents, if that God you speak about is the author of this filth.'

" 'Don't meddle with God again,' Ug told him. 'When you don't deny him, you insult him! What do you gain?'

" 'What do I gain? Nothing. I lose! I lose my time worrying again about the same thing we have to deal with as soon as Don Q appears though a door and begins to speak.'

" 'What's really serious for people like you, my dear Lu, is the disproportion between will and power. Between your reality and your ambition; between your pride and your capacity.'

" 'Yes,' Don Lu told me. 'A distance of death's size. I recognize it! Mister Don Q classified me: he found all the springs of my conduct. His skillful scalpel penetrated all the psychological layers and after having cut open this modest lover, he pontificated: "Disproportion between will and power!" Look: if my power were the same size as my will I would change the world from the bottom of its dirty underpants.'

" 'See?' I told him. 'You are nothing more than a poor confused reformist, an apostle without doctrine; a poor martyr without a cross.'

" 'Well,' Don Lu answered me, 'so what? And what if it is as you say? The situation doesn't change, anyway I am as I am: I don't want to be. Does it matter that you give me absurd names, that you qualify them, mix them up, throw them to the air; that you scatter them and pick them up again?'

" 'Words are important. Men are men because of words,' I said.

" 'Words are the most stupid way to emit bad breath, pure smelly air. You and your words.'

" 'I and my words,' I said. 'Yes, I and my words. Those words that come out one by one, consuming our time, enriching it, humanizing it. Words humanize time, they make it ours.'

" 'Oh! What an exquisite poet! Cheers!' Albert said. He returned to drink the last lukewarm beer in the house.

"Don Lu simply said: 'Bah!'

"There was an unexpected silence, which I resolved to break:

" 'Well,' I said to Lu. 'Why, if you admit the disproportion between your will and your power, don't you proceed intelligently suiting your will to your capacity for realization? This world is imperfect. Well! Why not better it? Why not do it employing the few forces we possess? There's so much to do! Look around you, and as soon as you look, you will find misery, a small or a large misery that perhaps you can remedy.'

" 'Look, my dear Q, to get this over with, I'm not qualified to be a social reformer, nor a martyr for the people's causes, nor any of those idiocies. For me, let capitalists, fascists, socialists, communists, and even anarchists blow up at the same time with their stupid aberrations. Regarding misery, you know very well that it horrifies me. It's one of the things I don't admit. Remember that miserable old man I found the day I was wearing brand new shoes . . .'

" 'Oh yes!' Albert interrupted. 'Lu Gautama Buddha came out from his walls, he saw the world horrified, and he sat in search of Nirvana!' "

CHAPTER XXVI: *Through the "Little Old Man of Misery" the Theme of Nirvana Is Explored, with Other Frankly Buddhist Reflections. Another Frustrated Suicide Is Incidentally Discussed.*

("LISTEN, Don Q," I interrupted him, "what is this about 'the old man of misery'?"

"It was," Don Q, told me, "one of the first conscious encounters that Don Lu had with life. He lived almost locked up in his house. One day he had to go out to see his brother who was in the hospital with a bullet in his chest, accused of having a suicide pact with a girl. Of course, that brother of Don Lu's, whom I am not even going to name, was even more radical. He got, from facts and not just attitudes, to the bottom of things. He had shot himself trying to hit his heart, but as he was lying on his left elbow and next to the girl who had just killed herself with the same pistol, the bullet didn't enter the heart; it went through the body and he didn't die. He only let his beard grow. And when he woke up, one night as I was watching him (of course, I remember I was reading Aeschylus, holding the book under a thin ray of light that entered through the half-opened door, a ray that only illuminated two or three lines so that I had to move the book, positioning the lines I was reading so that they could be lit by the ray. It was then that I became very aware of the terrible limitation that even Aeschylus faced to join one word and another to make ideas, to say things, and of the terrible tribute that beauty or truth pay to time) . . . He woke up, saw me and started to speak to me."

"Listen, Don Q," I interrupted him, "it must be a suicidal family . . ."

"No," he answered me, "it was a family of 'nonsuicides,' because this one didn't die and neither did Don Lu. Let me continue:

"The wounded man told me with a painful laugh (after describing to me a delirious dream in which he felt that he'd fallen from bed and inundated the room until he found me reading Aeschylus under a little ray of light), that the bullet had been the most painful and unpleasant gesture of courtesy he had ever received in his life, because—he told me—the girl was obsessed with suicide and he, partly to conquer her, partly to follow along to see how far she got, kept up the suicide line until they made a pact that he thought she'd never keep; but to his surprise, the very same night he conquered her and in the same bed, according to their agreement, she grabbed the pistol and serenely, sweetly, shot herself in the heart. He, after thinking about it for a while, understood he couldn't leave her alone, and greeting her, took the pistol, put it on the chest where he supposed the heart was and, bang! He told me this in a low tone, but deeply amusing. 'So, Q, you can see where courtesy can lead you and what you get from the "ladies first" deal'."

"Listen, Don Q," I interrupted him, "what an odd case, and how rapidly you tell it to me! On the other hand the one about Don Lu has taken some time, and if you think about it, it might be less interesting."

"Well," Don Q told me, "there's more plot in the one I've just told you, but it does set up deeper questions about the given word, which forced someone who loved life, admittedly in a rather sinister way, to discharge a shot toward himself by his own will, without feeling like it, just to agree with his very peculiar conscience . . ."

"That might be so," I told him, "although if we had chosen that tale as the main one we would still be on the pact, I think."

"Don't make fun of me! Remember I told you this because of the old man of misery, who is also a character without importance, but with subtlety, because with it you will understand Don Lu's temperament. You will see. I will tell it to you as he told it to me, by opening a parenthesis:

"Don Lu was still too young, still naive. But his fundamental attitudes were being established. At that time, forced to go out to see his brother, he returned with his new shoes full of mud. On seeing them, I asked him the compelling question:

" 'How goes it? What happened to you?'

" 'I have,' he told me, 'my shoes full of misery, pierced with horrible misery, the incredible misery that I have just seen. That misery that you, Q, with your happy irresponsibility, call "cosmic necessity," but that confronted as reality is unbearable. I hate it! I was on my way to the hospital,' Lu began to tell me. 'I suddenly entered a narrow street marked by low and narrow houses. Suddenly, all the world's misery fell on me: stony, muddy, covered by black waters, thick, stepped-on, pestilent, they made flaccid waves with each new bit of dirt that fell on them and slowly went to the bottom of the deep waters, which made waves that came and went, centering on a bubble that burst into a slow and dirty muck. Puddles, and where there were none, mud, which was a thicker puddle because it had more garbage. Mud, garbage, filth, saturated hoggishness, sprinkled, extending like pimples and crusts that exhaled a thick loose odor that floated in the air, that almost couldn't be seen and stayed, sticky, in the throat. Narrow doors, dirty, almost falling, that let me see, like papillae burst by infection, repulsive interiors in the most perfect of all miseries, everything soaking itself in that dense atmosphere, slow and sticky, whitish, which confused hallucination of darkness with the promiscuous. It blurred the broken windows, patched with opaque spider webs that served as the duct's cradle, or as sepulchres for the corpses of flies . . .

" 'Q, all the world's misery in one single street! And dirtying even more that painting which I had never seen nor imagined, women and pot-bellied children with rotten stomachs and glassy eyes behind which one could only guess there were pestilent puddles.

" 'In that painting, at the edge of the pavement, with his feet in the mud and the garbage, there was that horrible sick old man.

" 'He was all misery and in addition he was old.

" 'He was seated, curled up, looking at the world with his bleary eyes.

" 'They were horrible, sick, dirty old eyes. Miserable! Eyes in which the gelatinous gray corner invaded the pupil in morbid relaxation. Eyes that saw the world behind a mud screen, saw the world as bad, ugly, gray, smelly. I believe he must have confused objects with his stinking breath and he only looked at them because, in spite of all, his eyes worked: without interest, without repugnance, not even with resignation. It was a stupid, miserable old look!

" 'I don't think he found out that I, who passed by his side, was a clean, well-dressed, healthy young man who skipped puddles for fear of soiling my new shoes. Q, what impressed me most is that he didn't even ask for charity. I don't believe he could have asked for anything. That's how miserable he was! Nevertheless, those gelatinous eyes had a spark which shone anxiously and egotistically. I became aware that this old carcass wanted to be, be, be, even though it might be nothing more than a crust of misery. It was a repulsive tragedy, you can believe me: the desire, the necessity to be and persist, to be old and miserable, and to not even ask for charity.

" 'I felt a terrible anguish and a tremendous rage.

" 'I felt like pinching myself and caressing his poor old head which I saw was full of crusts.

" 'At the same time I felt like—like really kicking him hard, with all my might, like destroying him.

" 'I did neither. I didn't even throw him a coin.

" 'I ran away, anguished by the spectacle and hatefully remembering the coldness that you have pontificated so many times, telling me that "misery is a cosmic necessity," with that tone of feigned, meritless, abstract resignation that makes you understand everything. But within me, inside my passion, something broke forever and wanted to become undone with tears. A young man with new shoes who rebels and who only feels like crying, and he didn't even cry! Is crying all that's left, Q? Only crying and pontificating about the necessity of misery so that by contrast its contrary can exist, as you say many times in that self-reliant tone? Look, Q', Don Lu then told me, 'with all my might I ask never to see that old man of misery again. I want, with all my cowardice, to ignore misery, to ignore it, crusts, gray hairs, even rotten bellies. I swear,' he concluded, 'that I will never again see that little old man of misery.' He then picked up his dirty shoes and threw them to the street."

CHAPTER XXVII: *More Reflections on Nirvana and the Renunciation of the Tremendous Error of Ieity.*

"LISTEN, Don Q. Don Lu was younger then. Undoubtedly, Albert correctly associated him with that anecdote attributed to the Gautama Buddha. Don't you think so?"

"Yes," he replied. "It was a similar pretext. The Buddha, to the surprise of his brutal and sordid world, renounced the flesh, the world, and action. He contemplated the navel of the universe freeing himself from the terrible burden of personality. He renounced the I. He was a being, undoubtedly superior, but without the problems of Ieity. He renounced them."

"How odd," I observed. "How odd that men, made the same way and from the same substance, resolve important problems so differently: your Indians, Don Q, by sacrifice; the others, by establishing techniques of forgiveness; and Gautama . . ."

"Yes, Don Pepe, yes. Everything fits into the mystery. I have told you many times that, undoubtedly, the universe turns every wheel and fills the inexhaustible purse of all possibilities. Things do not return as that madman Nietzsche thought. Suppose it would be possible to admit that time ends because the possibilities, the probabilities, and the possible combinations of both also end. Only then could the universes repeat the cycle; but then it would be repeating infinitely, and an infinitely repeated infinite is absolute immobility . . ."

"Listen, Don Q," I interrupted him, "don't tire me with those gray buzzes, as you call them. That way only returns, as other times did, to the immobile motor of the Greeks and the saints. Let's separate perfection from imperfection, the Creator from his creatures in the most incomprehensible situation that can be set up. You correctly call it the gray buzz, as death must be."

"Look, Pepe," Don Q continued, "don't be afraid of these things. They are so important that they make up the source of every right to believe. They vindicate all faiths, or better yet, the great faith. But of all the reactions against the mystery, one of the ones that bother me most is the Buddha and his renunciation of deity. Note that he isn't suicidal as Don Lu pretended to be (behold the comparison among attitudes probably motivated by equivalent causes). Ultimately for Don Lu, the error was in the not-so-perfect creation. For Buddha the error was in the I's personality; from that arose, not protestation against, but rather meditation on the essential. And the essential is the stupor of the immobile that is almost nothingness, a personal will that renounces the I; a will that is not wanted; that is not even denied; a simple will in order to let oneself go. The error lies in existing as a person, that is, as the center of the universe's representation and its imperfections. A quiet effort to fuse into the notorious impersonality of immobility, which is as valuable as abandoning the infinite and its interminable source of inconsequences.

"In this way, undoubtedly, it completes imperfection, misery, pains, mistakes, because the personal conscience, which knows or recognizes the possibilities and vices of a universe that builds on the penetration of opposites and the dynamism of self-denying negation, can disappear or want to disappear. If you look carefully, it's the abandonment of dialectics (not its contradiction). It can originate in a moral position against the imperfect universe; but it's also the abandonment of all morals, as far as the conduct of the being that becomes responsible for it. It is, as I told you, to put aside personality's terrible duties; to renounce the Ieity's compromises.

"Ieity," Don Q continued, "is undoubtedly the source, the origin of almost every question: because there are beings, centers of conscience and conduct, there are injustices, miseries, pains, faults. Thus, there's also good will, joy, and merit. It's not unjust that stones fall and that gases disperse. A galaxy does not feel the return of its cycles nor does a sun suffer because it is consumed.

"Only the person, only the I, is the bearer of anxiety, defiance, and the sense of justice. The world had to, it does not mean God had to, believe in Ieity in order to contemplate in that mirror its greatness and its misery. Only because there's a personal being who suffers, who gets old and has ulcers and scabs, can the Gautama amaze himself; that stones are old and have lichen and that nothing happens. It's in the I that the universe includes the whole gamut of infinite imperfections. It's the I that protests, that judges or resigns itself. Pay attention Josefo. Pay attention! There is Buddha's terrible and unfathomable profundity: no pain, no love, no justice, no injustices. Why judge? To judge whom? To rectify whom? Blaspheme against whom?

Nothing, simply nothing: renounce the tremendous error of Ieity. To merge oneself, abandoning all kinds of will, even good will, into the final settlement of all wrongs and rights, which would create a harmonious equilibrium if there weren't intermediate beings that suffer or enjoy them. The great, immovable, final settlement in Buddha's navel.

"What a great solution: to end that fountain of all disagreement, the I! How many times, bachelor, how many times I tried to blend myself into the absolute spirit, contemplating my navel and sitting in the lotus position, and I only got pains in my joints and protests from the only things that are untransferable and definitely mine: my ego and my will, good and bad."

"Listen, Don Q, you must not have looked like a Buddha, who after all was a bit on the heavy side, but more like a carnival fakir, and as for your navel, I hardly believe one would be able to see much in that misery you call a stomach," I dared jest.

"Don't be funny, Pepe, don't be funny. These are serious questions that are important to millions of beings who have been, are, and will be, and who, somehow, assume some attitude before the mystery."

CHAPTER XXVIII: *On How Human Generation Belongs to Lucifer, with Other Transcendental Excesses.*

"YOU speak a lot about the mystery; but tell me, Don Q, honestly, what do you think about that question?"

"Think. I don't think. If you notice, it's not a problem of

thought; it's a problem of will. It's not thought, because it's not a matter of understanding the Universe, or comprehending it, which is thought's pretension. It's not a matter of fusing oneself but of confusing oneself in it. It is, you must realize, a problem of will. But understand well, it is not the Good Will of Christ, Our Lord (about which we will speak some other time, if I dare), the Good Will that is fitted into the irreducible responsibility of the personal man before his fellowmen. It's rather the will to abandon the will to be I. And that, occasionally, attracts me as the solution to the Ieity's anxieties. But other times it seems to me to be a horrible betrayal of the world of Lucifer and Judas, to whose great generation somehow belong Humanity and its salvation through its will and from its own conduct. It is then that I accept all the seriousness of time and I feel like a strip coagulated with infinity that, due to its own will, is weaving itself on the road of the two halves, from our Indians' Omeyocan, from the 'Second Place,' between the 'Second Place,' accepting responsibility, the burden and the joy of infinite imperfections, and in them and for them to follow the Ieity which brought Lucifer to hell, Judas to suicide, and us probably to salvation. (I think that it may be better to lose our I. It is then that the horrendous gray buzz arrives.)"

"Listen, Don Q, I strongly protest! What is this about human generation somehow belonging to Lucifer? Listen! No! Don't confuse things! Don't be so complicated!"

"Don't be scared, Josefo, no matter what, we would still be God's children. Don't be scared! Or better yet, as my good uncle Antonio * would say: 'Be not obstreperous!' Be not obstreperous, my good Josefo, be not obstreperous! I

* You see that savage Don Q also called himself Antonio Machado's nephew.

firmly believe that that great rebel was the first perfectly free creature to leave his Creator's hands and was so much in his own image that he indicted him, as I already have told you and now repeat, not for that, but because I think it was then that the generation of I's was created that, just for the fact of being that, are distinct, and because they're free they can suffer and be miserable, or have fun and be rich, in their own opporunity, an opportunity that, at least as far as its own time and space, is perfect, irremissibly theirs (ours, better said), and not even the Creator would be able to take that opportunity from him under penalty of subverting the order and betraying himself. In that betrayal, neither with merit nor any fault, another sort of Lucifer would have emerged. Before I told you it was due to pride. Now I complete it for you: it was also due to Ieity. The first being to become anxious about Ieity was Lucifer. The human genre was created after that experience, full of large and small I's, all potential rebels, seed of great protests, owners of all misery, all the world's pain and joy, because for that you have to be an I, or there's nothing more than the Lord's boredom."

"For God's sake! Don't scare me, Don Q, don't confuse me so much. You're turning out to be more satanic than Don Lu."

"Don't be an idiot, Pepe, don't be an idiot! I simply state the facts. You have to admit that the infinite's only limit, as I have told you, is the I, which has the quality of wholeness. To that degree the I is also God's only limit. It is so true that Lucifer probably rebelled because of that, and that humanity suffers and protests for the same reason or it resigns itself. That's why there are revolutions, in heaven and on earth, because there are unhappy I's. Man with his free conscience was a risky invention. A dangerous and subversive invention. If not, tell me why and how someone is saying these things. Let's see, Josefo, let's see. Think . . ."

I positively refused to think and told him:

"Look, Don Q, my head hurts and my ears are ringing. I don't understand, and what's more, I don't want to understand all these rare things you are telling me. It's better that we go on with Don Lu and his suicide. You stopped where Albert observed that the rejection of misery made Don Lu a sort of Gautama."

"All right, I'll go on," Don Q told me, and he did in this way:

CHAPTER XXIX: *The Suicide Tale Continues, with Some Reflections on the Universe's Idiotic Imperfections Before Paradise Was Lost.*

" 'MY opportune Albert," Don Lu answered him, 'there's no way through which you can make me responsible for Nirvana, which is a compromise I neither accept nor understand. What I want and have always wanted, I will repeat it so all of you can understand it, is not a Nirvana foreign to my temperament; not even Grace, which would be more in agreement with me, if I could believe in a personal God and forgive the idiotic imperfections of the universe. What I want is leisure, as a meadow of my liking that, get it straight, must be real and free. Do you understand, Don Q? You, who somehow have Spanish blood in your veins. Do you understand that what I want is the perfection of leisure and desire?'

" 'Of course I understand you,' I answered him." (Don Q

is speaking, don't think it's me. I don't understand a thing about that.) " 'Because I'm partly Spanish and Indian . . .' "

" 'Then explain to this Teutonic clod why I don't feel like doing it. You can't deny me that I'm opening for you a beautiful vein so that you can extract a huge amount of words.' "

" 'I thank you for it,' I humbly answered him." (Don Q continues to speak, I clarify that because the bit about humility might confuse him with myself.) " 'I thank you for it because within it there is an interesting framework for the theme of the leisure's firm will, which, if we think about it, we will find to be the will to find paradise lost.'

" 'Bravo,' Don Lu interrupted me. 'Although you're somehow repeating yourself, it is a beautiful and opportune repetition. It's true! That's why I wanted you to speak. Do you see, Albert, you idiot, how the young master is opening for you a possibility of understanding, which your unbearable German stuffiness will surely not understand? It's exactly what's happening to me! I recognize it with joy. You're an authentic prophet who opportunely says what we want you to say. You are a prophet! Long live Don Q! That's what I have, a firm leisure will, grasped by my willingness for paradise, with which my umbilical cord is about to break.'

"Extremely flattered by Don Lu's warm acceptance, I continued exploring in that rich vein:

" 'There's a private logic in your conduct, Don Lu; even your rejection of guilt fits perfectly. You want to live in a world previous to guilt, which is precisely paradise, before work, before the sweat that repulses you. A world without the penalty of work is precisely the world of leisure. And that's paradise, the kingdom of leisure, where desire is real. Magnificent! I'm also enthusiastic, Don Lu, because I'm understanding your problem. I will probably kill myself too.'

"Ug took me seriously. He gave me a poke and said:

" 'You! So bright, so intelligent. You don't respect anything. You're always playing games. It's a shame that you don't know how important life is and how beautiful it is to live in God's fear and respect!'

" 'Bravo, Ug! Now you are the Angel of Paradise,' Albert said. 'Throw them out for being disrespectful. They now have knowledge and they play with it as if it were a ball, especially Q, who remained as broom Angel. Throw them out! Go on!' And he pushed him as if he wanted him to take the flaming sword.

" 'Don't touch me with your dirty hands full of tapeworms,' Ug answered him violently. 'Now I don't understand what's happening. It's Q who now speaks about suicide and this skinny reject is tempting me as if he were the devil, so that I may do things that I don't understand why they should be done or why we should make fun of sacred things. I believe that among all of us here the truly evil one is this skinny drunk because he is envious and very dangerous. He shuts his mouth and waits for the opportunity to get a leg-hold. He never gives his opinion, he only picks and feels. It's all right that I don't give my opinion because I don't understand very well the troubles you are in. I believe in God, in the Virgin Mary, and in the Holy Spirit. I believe in the sanctity of work and in all those things you know. It saddens me that you speak of the Bible as if it were a movie. You're so difficult!' Saddened, he kept quiet, I believe because he had spoken so much. But he was so sincere that I had to take him seriously, I told him:

" 'No, my old Ug, I'm simply speaking to understand Lu and his reasons. We are not disrespectful. Deep inside we agree with you, we simply are hurt by things you are not. So as not to fight with what hurts us we pretend to play with important things, to take importance away from them. But notice how understanding is Don Lu's attitude of loving Paradise. The problem is not that his will looks for paradise but rather that, not reaching it, it prefers to go to hell.'

" 'That's what I've told him many times!' Ug heatedly told me. 'That! but not with those words. That's what I feel. It is as if Lu were still a boy who doesn't want to learn to be a man.'

"Don Lu looked at Ug with much surprise; but he had the good sense to keep quiet while I continued:

" 'You see, Ug, how we somehow are in agreement. The closest thing to paradise, through leisure and even willingness, is, no doubt, a happy childhood, and Don Lu had a happy one. It's in that stretch between infancy and serious life that Lu is losing paradise.'

" 'That's a crude explanation,' Lu said. 'It sounds like psychiatry. Soon the complexes will come out, Oedipus and those other monsters from Freud and his mother. That's how we get to boredom and the interpretation of dreams . . .'

"I wanted to recover lost ground and, without much enthusiasm, I said:

" 'How complexly beautiful is the world of the human being! Through how many ways can will overflow and how interesting it would be to compare Paradise and Nirvana! The first, with men who give names to things that live with the whole world at their service, and spend time as they desire; while the second is void of men and surely void of time and transformations.'

" 'You may be right, Q,' Lu told me, 'but, as usual when you feel you have corraled me with your thoughts, that in no way changes the situation. Perhaps it explains it, but it does not change my determination. One thing is what has happened and why, and another very different one is what will happen, which has its own reason in the future and unattached to the past. I'd like to suppose you are right: that my childhood was my paradise and that I have resolved not to let go of it. That, I insist, in no way changes my problem. It simply makes it smaller. But it does not change the essence of my determination.'

" 'Of course!' I answered him. 'You can put paradise wherever the hell you like, such is its condition. Of course it doesn't change it.'

" 'Well!' Ug interrupted us. 'All this I've been hearing for some time means that despite all that has been said things are as they were in the beginning. Right? In that case I want all of you to tell me what the hell your intelligence is good for? You talk and talk. Go up, down, one way, the other, you go down again . . . You don't understand, you agree, you disagree, talk some more, and . . . what do you come to? You are always on roads that lead nowhere.'

" 'The roads that lead nowhere are the ones that, sometimes, allow us to find that which we haven't lost,' I said, sententiously, taking Ug seriously.

" 'You see, Q? What have you said with so many words? . . . Nothing about nothing. You tie yourself into knots!' "

CHAPTER XXX: *On How, by Tying Ourselves Into Knots, We End Up As Spiral Galaxies. Some Reflections on Merit and Suckers.*

"LISTEN, Don Q, I think that somehow old Ug was right. And I also think that you're tying yourself into a knot, except that if you don't like the world I will change it to 'sphere,' which is more to your liking, or if I must, to 'spiral galaxies.' Am I not right?"

"You're right, Josefo, you're right. As a matter of fact I'm tying myself into spheres and galaxies. What an excellent phrase! You can see how important words are. We change 'knots'—a vulgar, elementary, everyday expression which pertains to smallness—to 'sphere,' which gives the idea of stellar space. The qualifier pleases me: 'Don Q, the one who ties himself up in spheres.' 'Don Q, the one who becomes a spiral galaxy!' Yes sir, what a wonder! How keen you're turning out to be!"

"Except, my dear Don Q, that Ug was not keen at all and he simply said 'Q, the one who ties himself into knots.' "

"And he's also right," Don Q said, "and I told him so:

" 'Ug, it's true, I tie myself up into knots. Do you know what's wrong with these things we think about? That we all leave from the same point to get to the same place, except that we take a long, winding road and others stay in the same place and sooner or later we find them there. Either we are all correct or no one is.' "

" 'Listen, Q,' Albert interrupted, 'it now seems that even that hairy beast Ug is beating you with a broom.'

" 'You're right,' I told him.

"Ug evidently became enthusiastic with Albert's observation and told us:

" 'It's really great that I don't know much about anything, nor about so many problems or entanglements. I know that paradise must be gained by behaving well. It's like a prize for good conduct, which is . . .'

" 'A good business,' Albert interrupted.

" 'I don't know whether I care if it is or it isn't a good business; all I know is that it has to be deserved. I think it's something like justice.' " (It was obvious that Don Q was trying to reproduce the exact, rather awkward expressions made by Ug). " 'At least I think I wouldn't be comfortable in a free paradise, and if I weren't pleased, it wouldn't be paradise. Am I wrong?'

" 'Of course you are!' Lu interrupted him, 'Of course you're wrong! As whenever you try to think! Adam got to paradise naked. Newly created, he received everything just for the hell of it, for he was the king of creation. It was a condition of his lordship. I still have serious doubts about his character, except for my acceptance that paradise is given freely, because otherwise Albert would be right: it's a good business, not only in the long run but in long installments. At least, in my case, I not only do not conceive, I do not even admit paradise in a way that is not gratuitous, in the same way I received my childhood, just to anticipate Q's observation. And obviously such an easy solution, a free paradise as Ug says in his idiocy, which in this case is right, is not a situation that admits this complicated world of merits and contrasts. I reaffirm my decision to get off the list of those who deserve the lost paradise.'

" 'Certainly then, for I'm not a king, or a duke, or a marquis, only a man of flesh and bone, and I believe that paradise, or whatever you want to call it, has to be gained—if not, it isn't worth it. It wouldn't be a manly endeavor, but rather for babies: "Come on, here's your pacifier, don't cry . . ." ' Upon saying this, Ug blushed, frightened at his own daring.

" 'Wow! What a sweep!' Albert exclaimed.

" 'Bravo, Ug!' I said and dared to add, 'You have set up a question of great depth, which I take to be Western man's tragedy in his moral world . . .'

" 'If you're going to start with your little speeches, I'll start screaming until I get my pacifier,' Lu had the good nature to promise.

"All of us celebrated the tribute given to Ug's sincere ingenuity. He, contrary to his custom and undoubtedly stimulated by his unexpected successes, told us:

" 'Friends! At least this one time I have been given importance and my things have been celebrated, so let the great Don Q embellish them.'

" 'OK, but make it brief!' Lu said. Albert laughed.

"A bit taken by the acute timing with which he accepted my audience, under other conditions I would have remained quiet; but being that it was a matter of gaining time and saying things that were interesting, irritating or boring, situations that in one way or another refer to life, I continued with all naturalness:

CHAPTER XXXI: *Serious Reflections on Sin and Other Matters Ending in "-ity." Some Talk on the Conscience Between "Always" and "Never" So As to Accumulate the Nothings We Have Been.*

" 'WELL, I believe that Western man has converted his conduct, intentions as well as behavior, into a moral problem that turns around the idea of sin, which the Indian world ignored because what mattered in it was how to die, not so much how to live. It was just to keep universal order, not so that the human being may have transcendence.' " ("I won't repeat," Don Q told me, "some things that I added, because in some ways I have explained them to you at other times.") " 'In the Oriental Buddhist world, which is not interested in the behavior problem due to its quiet tendency to confuse the I with what it supposes to be the universal essence . . .' " ("I also won't tell you," Don Q repeated, "some embellishments that I placed in that conversation concerning this idea, for I recently spoke to you on this theme.") . . ." 'everyone's moral compromises do not establish a direct relation with the human being. They accept another transcendence. On the other hand, the Western attitude is radically different: human conduct in its entirety becomes a moral problem between the person and divinity, whose transcendence is personal fault or merit and, consequently, punishment or glory. Notice how those basically egotistical expositions, always based on the Ieity's transcendentality against the "alterity" of divinity . . .'

" 'I protest!' Don Lu interrupted me, frankly irritated and almost screaming. 'Forgive me, but separately I cannot stand those pedantic words ending in that loose "-ity" form, and together they become unbearable.

" 'I don't believe I have done anything to deserve such a punishment and I state, under oath, that I'm not about to listen to a dissertation which, from the way it looks, threatens to be too direct for my total lack of "patientiality." Therefore, with Ug's permission, let's bring this lively chat to an end, for it's soon going to be midnight . . .'

" 'Oh yes! The thing about the "crystality" slipper and all that,' Albert commented."

CHAPTER XXXII: *Concerning Some Themes for a European Cenacle on the Unfathomable Reserve of Ideas, Together with Reflections on Western Culture's Attitudes Towards Responsibility and Other Equally Jewish Themes.*

"LISTEN, Don Q, it's a shame that they didn't let you go on with a theme that promised to be so interesting. Although I must agree with Don Lu that that business about the Ieity's transcendentality, 'alterity,' and the rest, was too much for the situation, as you had once before happily thrown out some other theme . . . It would have become too conventional had you ripped yourself to pieces expounding on a theme like that. I really believe that only you can imagine such things."

"The thing is that precisely at that moment words started to form, and ideas that had been going around my head for a long time, and it was not the time to lose the opportunity."

"Yes, Don Q," I answered, "but now you don't even bother with it! How and where did you believe that at that moment you were going to have an audience for such an elevated theme, really a theme for something like a select European cenacle or for an Ethics class or something. Lu's repulsion was perfectly natural, what's worse, it wasn't the first time . . . Besides, I noticed that you were losing points. Nevertheless, we should chat about those themes that truly interest me, although it can't be denied that by being important they are rather boring. But they should be considered at least once in a lifetime."

"I would have to make an effort to get into the swing of things," Don Q told me, "but, as I already told you, they were things that were becoming words for me. It's odd, Pepe, that you have things inside you that you are not aware of and you don't know how they got there. Inside ourselves we have enormous, unfathomable reserves of ideas, feelings, and emotions that suddenly, due to an occurrence, a stimulus, an opening, even by an effort, begin to melt through words and that, by drops or spurts, start coming out, much to your surprise. Including what I'm telling you this moment. Where did I get it? How did it come to me? Did someone tell it or dictate it to me? How did that vague and undetermined expression, which I'm understanding little by little as it becomes words, form inside of me? It seems as if there were a common fund of things that are everywhere and suddenly you plug them in and you make them yours when you put them in your own words. As a lawyer, I don't know whether you understand. I believe words are the property title for ideas. One would have to scream with Jean-Jacques, the first to put ideas into words, and say, 'these are mine.' He found naive people who believed it, and he greatly damaged humanity. How many crimes could have been avoided if, without words, someone could have said (how absurd!) 'Don't believe him! He's a charlatan! Ideas belong to one and all!' Only words belong to someone, and they are air!"

"Listen, Don Q, what odd ideas you have. While you were saying them, and without knowing why, I bet you don't know what image came to my mind? You want me to tell you? I don't know why but I remembered a section of the road from Pueblo to Mexico just before one goes up the mountains that separate the neighboring valleys. It's a straight stretch of land with huge trees that during the

night—my memory is nocturnal—appeared from afar as vague contours faintly hinted at by my car's headlights, which rescued them from obscurity. Soon they became rigid profiles of branches that rapidly became domes in the night, to be lost above, on the roof of my car, and returned to the obscurity that remained behind, like the one in front, merged into one with the car's speed. Don Q, did I say something wrong?"

"No," he answered, "it was a graphic expression that was about to turn poetic. It would be vulgar on my part if I were to tell you that it's a simile connected to what I was telling you, which doesn't really interest me because of its vagueness. But what we have said has stimulated me to give in to your request . . ."

(Note that I never had to beg him for anything.)

". . . in such a way that I will try to put into words this vague mass that occurs, or resides, somewhere inside me. I will make it mine as long as I can give it the dimensions of my own words:

"I believe it interesting to be fully aware that man's conduct as a personal responsibility that bases itself on its liberty and transcends its destiny, is a peculiar attitude of Western culture, coming from its roots, particularly the Jewish ones. This has created a very special link between religion and morals. Religion becomes a moral problem for the human being, based on an original sin that may be expiated by punishment or pardon and one in which one can sin again to repeat the same cycle. A fundamental condition appears from that point of view, namely Western man's vocation for his own salvation as an acting person: the problem of conduct is saving oneself, as I have told you before. And that, Joseph, has been one of my anxieties, because that thought deprives conduct of disinterestedness and, automatically, of merit. You don't see it like that? It's going to be difficult to explain this to you who are so objective and, I believe, even skeptical.

"The simple fact that I have to use a traditional language is going to make things difficult, things that, as I have told you on other occasions, I would like to put into music. But now my duty is to put them into words. I have thought, especially in my long periods of solitude, that there must be some kind of pure conduct, totally alien to the idea of personal salvation, and including in this expression the same satisfaction for good behavior, the praise of merit itself. Suddenly what comes to mind is what I dare call the morbose race of reflections that displace one another until they take away my tranquillity completely: 'One should do this.' 'I have done it; I have the satisfaction of being good.' 'Don't do it for the satisfaction of being good.' 'But I thought so much about having and not having satisfaction.' And with this I remain totally convinced that I'm so, so extraordinarily good, that I'm capable of wanting to do good things for themselves, without their producing any satisfaction in me, which leaves me so satisfied that it leads me to rephrase the problem, only at another level, until I totally lose tranquillity, for among merits, salvations, satisfactions, interest, disinterest, interest for disinterest, etc., my sense of qualification becomes void and that horrifying race of morbose displacements, which I can't avoid when I begin to judge my own actions, starts. Is it not definitely disagreeable, my dear Josefo? And if I think I have to behave to save myself, I feel guilty about searching for my salvation, which is almost a painful physical punishment. And also because I can't admit my damnation because I find it unjust, I end up screaming that I need a judge of human conduct. Or is man so desperately alone in the universe that he doesn't even have a judge for his conduct? Aren't there any judges, as Lu screams to me when we touch on these matters? Isn't there a judge, Josefo, isn't there a judge to judge me? And then I think if I'm someone to have a judge, I must deserve him. Am I someone who deserves a judge? Is there a judge between the two halves? You don't understand me, Josefo, you don't understand me! You make unbearable idiotic faces! Or you look at me as if you were thinking 'this guy is crazy!' "

(I don't know why the great Don Q told me this, for I must admit he was beginning to move me, although I didn't quite understand his complicated frameworks, those displacements of qualification which lead him to vertigo. I chose to keep quiet and not make any remark. He then proceeded as follows:)

"How terrible it must be, if it is, to be the judge of merits! Where's merit? In total renunciation? In total unconsciousness? Is the Indian world right in ignoring it? Is the Buddhist world right? I have the need, the thirst to know what human conduct in the universe means! Do we weave cloths that someone contemplates? Does it coagulate somewhere? Is it good for anything? I have to know! Or simply, nothing happens and this little, transitory spark of my conscience naively runs from always to never, and what has just happened, what just happened to me, puff! becomes nothing. Where do the nothings we have been accumulate, Josefo, where? Where and when? The terrible thing that occurs to me when I get to this point—I tell you sincerely—you know what it is? That I definitely don't accept salvation as the motive of my conduct . . . the doubt remains in me that I could save myself, and with this my whole system is turned upside down. The error is probably in the Ieity, that possibility that had to realize itself in the world in order to fill the inexhaustible purse of possibilities. But what a terrible problem! It was as if a mirror had created another mirror in front of itself to reflect itself, and then the interminable imperfection of the infinite came out. I'm about to tell you, my dear Josefo, that God made himself imperfect when he made the I's mirror. I don't know exactly what I'm saying; but as you sometimes say, my esteemed lawyer: when saying and thinking these things, somewhere in the universe (or only in my head) static and short circuits are being produced. Don't you think so?"

"I not only don't think so, I don't even understand these confused things you are telling me. What I do understand is why Ug said you were tying yourself into knots, I mean, spheres . . ."

CHAPTER XXXIII: *Wherein Socrates Appears and I Speak of the Polis, the Acropolis, the Parthenon, the Agora, Columns, Tunics, and Other Frankly Hellenic Reflections, to Conclude with the Usual Crossroads and the Infinite Persistence of Imperfection and the Permanent Occurrence of All Possibilities.*

"YES," he told me, "I get myself into tremendous spheres; but it's due to my Ieity's condition and I cannot, nor do I want, to renounce it. It would be tasty, after all, to solve the problem like Don Lu, or to not bother with it at all, like Ug. But deep inside I'm pretty conservative, even conforming. I must tell you, I accept the order of things and with all my heart I admit that time passes by and changes me. Maybe someday I will become a fairly serious lawyer, like you for example, with your mashed-up face and your 'I only know that I know how to make briefs and how to answer demands as time goes by until the hour of my death, amen' expression, which is, of course, much more comfortable than the Socratic way. Socrates at least knew he didn't know, from which no doubt also came that morbose vertigo that finally led him to accept the hemlock and to keep until the very end his generous doubt that 'it's time for us to leave, you (the judges) that you may live, I, to die. Between you and me, who is better off?' Ah, good old Socrates! How I love him! Some day I will go to the old Agora to cry for Socrates . . ."

"Listen, Don Q, you make me dizzy. Just look at you jumping all over the place. Suddenly, and through a strange association of ideas, you are already with Socrates and want to be in the old Agora. Well, I must inform you that I—I and not you, be it known—went and sat on a stone, facing the Acropolis, and I even cried for Socrates. You want me to tell you about it? If you allow me I will tell you with more or less the same words that I told it to my sons. Is that all right with you?"

Reluctantly, Don Q, who was rather exalted, accepted my proposition, most of all when he found out that some of the things I thought about had been inspired by things he had told me.

It is because of Don Q's acceptance that I dare to impose on you some of my personal impressions. But I couldn't let the opportunity go by. You no doubt understand. Don't you?

"Look, Don Q: I arrived in Athens (I begin there because

I'm sure you will recognize yourself in some of my emotions). You know, looking at my old maps. Athens was a point on a chart. I travel thousands of miles, cross the sea, gain time from time itself. I get to the Polis, houses, faces, different words. I sit on a stone of the Parthenon, I pick up a small stone, and again Athens is a point, now between my hands. I was in the Polis, the one from my General Theories of the State classes, the one from my textbook. The Polis in which everything originated.

"I must tell you, Don, that I fearfully reached the disillusionment of what was eagerly awaited. But I became aware that elementary purity keeps the mystery of its greatness. I was afraid of meeting Socrates' environment. I was afraid that my reason and my emotion would overcome the frame of reality which, idealized, would break on impact.

"But fortunately it wasn't like that.

"Two intense moments of tearful emotion (Don Q, I tell you that without blushing, trusting that you understand me). Just two very small fractions of time in which one makes contact with the universe. Just two seconds that are worth a whole life; those unforgettable moments of now and ever, my life's quintessence. I have lived them before (you will understand it well, Don Q, by listening to Beethoven, reading Shakespeare or the Book of Job, walking through Oaxaca, Veracruz, Jalisco. I have understood the messages of men and of Teuhtlampa, and yours, Don Q: the expression that signifies art, that transmission of spherical essences (notice, Don Q, spherical, not ball-like) in an infinite universal movement (do you see?) from in and out and from outside toward everywhere. Two moments, both associated with the Acropolis.

"The first occurred when I got back from the first obligatory visit, on a tour, the industrialization of someone else's curiosity that converts a group into something like a herd that moves to the sounds of the Light Cavalry." (Don Q smiled). "I was returning, and from the first portico (the Propileus?) I looked up and found myself, for the first time although I had already seen them, with the column. With the column's essence. With the archetype made of stone, the elementary matter of our material universe. I understood it. I saw man's presence in our sphere: above the piled-up rough stones, elementary, tight, inert, shining, and even humble. From the primal matter, from the same stone, the Parthenon is made, columns made by man above the stone sphere. Human order. The world, man's own sphere that climbs and extends until it is harmony, and harmony becomes stone. It coagulates in a vibrant rhythm, at the same time intense and quiet, serene and sublime. That's man, Don Q, another order above the natural. The factory of a better world, intentional, voluntary, responsible, beautiful . . ."

(Here Don Q looked at me curiously, if not with some interest, as if asking himself, is it truth?)

". . . stone columns, built stone on stone, to detain prayer and begging, to stop the rational triangle of mystery which is spherical . . ."

"Listen, Don Pepe," Don Q interrupted me, "from what I'm hearing, you also have a frank and excessive affection for spheres, as if you liked the little word. Your mouth fills up. I'm not criticizing you! It's fine! It's fine! Go on."

"The frontispiece above the sphere and among the spheres, Don Q—just so you can see how far I've taken many of your concepts—the column, the pure, white, bright, quiet, vibrant columns, there, behind the light, in the middle of our universe, like long candles that only time has set on fire and that will be consumed by the weight of gazes."

"Listen, Don Pepe, you are not as dry as you appear.

What you tell me, it seems, has too many spheres and adjectives, it sounds tolerable . . ."

I went on:

"Above a stone world, man's work raised: by beauty, by the cult of mystery. A link with the spirit, petrified in harmony. Serenity before destiny, which later on turns dynamic in the tunic. Column and tunic, Greece's Spirit. The direct line, repeated in parallels, which combined in the infinite or in movement and which end wherever beauty desires it, because it can end where the Greek wanted it to end. Above the rough stone, the emotion of the stone being made a hymn, prayer, conjunction of love and rhythm, with the precise scale between the column, men, and gods.

"The Parthenon: I felt it for a second, Don Q: just one, but it was sublime, intense, and now, years later, I turn it into analysis, words, and uneasiness."

(Don Q looked at me curiously.)

"The other moment, Don Q, was also at the Acropolis, seen from the old Agora, close to Theseus' Temple. There was the Agora, reduced to light, landscape, and Socrates' echo (that Socrates whom you love so much, Don Q). I raised my eyes and the Parthenon was there again, in its majestic simplicity, above the sacred mountain, sown by those mystical and sensual Mediterranean cypresses, a green flame with soft curves and sharp peaks. There was a bright and warm light between the Parthenon and me. In front, the Agora's ruins.

"Another second, Don Q, an intense one, which filled me and overflowed through my eyes in tears, light, and memory. Column and dialogue. The sacred tracks of the Panathenaea.

"Socrates, Socrates, Socrates, Socrates, Socrates, Socrates, in that very Agora full of humility and wisdom, where important words could be said without seeming either ingenuous or pedantic: Truth, Beauty, Harmony, Sanctity, Peace, Love. Each word, a column. Each ray of light a detained, vibrant dialogue, an eternal example of human spirit lifted from the earth and the rock, meeting the destiny of making columns and speaking words."

"Don Pepe, this is fine! A bit affected, but it sounds good!"

"Thanks," I told him, and went on:

"The old Agora, the Mediterranean sun, new laurels, reborn in every epoch, like the cycles of Dionysius resurrected, laurels identical to those of every era, now seen in the same light that illuminated Socrates. So, my dear Don Q, you are aware that I, your modest friend, have already cried for Socrates, in daylight and at the old Agora."

"Very interesting and descriptive," Don Q commented, "but it does not set up nor solve anything regarding what we were talking about. It was a parenthesis of dubious merit, which I accredit to you, my dear Josefo. There was a moment in which I expected more. Well. Let's go on with what's really important, leaving the anecdotal aside. Don't you think so?"

"Well, yes," I had to comment, feeling little for Don Q's firm determination for important and transcendental things.

"You are to live. I, to die. Between you and me, who is better off? What an old man! Don't you think so, Josefo? The closest thing to pure duty. A conduct without any certainty. An attitude firmly constructed on a doubt that redeems itself, to conclude that only the will matters, a good will, a formula that he didn't use, but that he deserved to have said. Look, my dear Pepe, I don't know through what curious association of ideas Socrates arrived at those moments in which I was giving you a show of great discomposure. The thing is that the Socratic is the other Western attitude, also responsible; but not necessarily transcended, but doubted and above all affirmed: 'things are holy because the gods want them, or the gods want them because they are holy.' You see, my good Josefo? And in spite of rational doubt, the straight determination of conduct: just a small piece of the world among so many infinite possibilities and a firm will to assert itself in behavior. What's behind? What was behind? What's in front? What will there be in front? Just a little piece, small and doubtful, illuminated by our conscience, kept by our conscience, projected by our imagination. A small gap among so many possible roads. But we affirm ours, exclusively ours, the one that leads us to want holy things because they are holy and nothing else. Salvation? What does it matter?"

"Listen, Don Q, I had never been aware of your Socratic vocation. What an interesting thought. I can see you now, dressed in a tunic. But the funny thing is I saw you with a big cloak and hat with a big feather, and a while ago I even imagined you looking (impossible hypothesis) at your belly. You really surprise me because I think you are basically sincere; but you explore so much, I think you must be very tired of jumping about."

"The thing is I know how to hear all human voices and they all tell me something and find some sort of resonance. That's why I live in this beautiful world of constant discoveries, even down to the one of everyday surprise at myself. The more I explore myself, the more I ignore myself. Spurts, sparks, and quarries, all of which I feel inside of me. I can never be still. But what probably worries me more is the value of conduct. You know, at times I think that, undoubtedly, the best way to solve the universe, one where the error of creating the I has been committed, our world's true original sin, would be for everything to end: that all memory must be erased and that in such a way there remain, nowhere, the greatness of accepted duty, of sanctity admitted because it's holy. May the world that our world has created disappear, better, much better than the other one, the one with falling stones, a world woven with our acts and only attached to our memory. You know? It's enough that memory end for History to end and for this world to go by and that its horrors and glories become nothing. Nothing. That would be enough. Do you see how narrow the Ieity's limits are?

"I think that its greatness lies precisely in that. In that precarious consistency. In that, its anguishing narrowness. Nothing more than memory to end sin, faults, merits. Our conduct is attached to that very subtle world. It also has the great audacity to assert its own order. Or are we simply unconscious vehicles in a great play in which we don't participate as authors? Is our order, the one we lift with our will, good or bad; is it simply another experience, done to exhaust another possibility in the interminable infinite chain of imperfections? Does the beauty we want and dream of reduce itself to that? Is there someone on our side who picks up our wishes, our emotions, our systems, and our works, and stores them as we store wheat? Is someone playing with us? If it were so, how enormous Socrates' greatness would be, and that of our Indians, who, in one way or another, took our game seriously and asserted themselves. If someone is playing with us, my dear Josefo, I will have to ask him: Between you who play and us who are played upon, who is better off?

"But no, other times I think everything is much more sordid and stupid than that. We are simply becoming entangled according to the law of the occurrence of all possibilities and now it is the turn of the one we mean to be, with all the implications that our possibility, having occurred, will move on. Or is it always occurring according to another law, the law of imperfection's infinite persistence?"

"Listen, Don Q," I interrupted him, "from what I gather, whichever road you choose to start traveling, sooner or later you find yourself at the crossroads of chirps, that neutral place where all your explorations are emptied. You will understand why I am so calm, surrounded by my world, which I am penetrating by means of steps that are always ready for laughter."

CHAPTER XXXIV: *Wherein I Intend to Demonstrate that Laughter Is the Great Savior of Human Dignity. You Will Know How to Laugh, My Son: A Great Human Laughter Filling the Horrendous Vacuum of Ether.*

"LISTEN, listen to me, Josefo, what's new about laughter . . . ?"

"That's something you haven't taught me, my dear and admired Don Q. I have learned that myself with time. While you chirp and come and go and find things you haven't lost and lose things that you already had, I have learned the wonderful lesson of laughter.

"You know, Don Q, of the few things I have gathered in life and that I don't owe to you is laughter. This wonderful possibility of laughing. I sincerely believe that laughter is the great savior of human dignity. 'And you will know how to laugh and dance in the midst of things.' That's how the naked human creature, pressed between two infinites, the small and the large, terrified by the mystery, barely grasping its history, almost in darkness, sometimes overwhelmed by pain, mistreated and absurd, can laugh to save its dignity. Laugh, Don Q. We can laugh at everything: at pain, at mystery, at our unprotected smallness or at the cosmos' greatness. We can laugh at the Milky Way, Don Q. Don't you see? We can laugh! With all respect I must tell you that not only have I learned to laugh at myself, but sometimes, with all considerations, I laugh at you, my wonderful and dear Don Q. I laugh at your tortures, your chirps, your generosity. Smile, Don Q, because you haven't learned to laugh at the infinite's infinitude. You only succeed at giving yourself pain!"

"I don't get the joke," Don Q answered me gloomily. "All that's happening to me is a serious thing. I think you laugh due to astonishment. You laugh due to ignorance. In the end, I don't know why you laugh. But if you think you rescue your ignorance by laughter, laugh, do whatever you want, I will continue exploring and looking for answers. I don't want laughter, Don Pepete, I don't want laughter. I want answers to my questions, and if I find them or if someone gives them to me, I'm going to feel so fulfilled that undoubtedly I'll want to explode to bring the answers to every corner of the world."

"Don't explode, Don Q, don't explode! Let out a great laugh, and may great laughter be the answer to all the questions that have no answer!"

"Wonderful!" Don Q said. "Now you turn out to be Don Pepe the Laugh-Riot. Not the dried-out Pepe I thought, but the one who laughs. Well! It's a poor, sad solution. It's what I call stupid laughter. Unheard of, to laugh! 'Laughter to save the human being's dignity.' Why? What are we going to rescue it from?"

"From the chirps, Don Q, the chirps and the short circuits. Just get to the edge, learn to laugh so that you can go on; laugh, Don Q, and go on living. Some day I will invite you to paint a huge painting that will be called 'Human Dignity's Great Laugh.' A great laugh in the middle of the Galaxies. What do you think, Don Q? A great human laugh filling the great vacuum of ether."

"Frankly it looks very discouraging," Don Q said. "I hope I don't end up laughing. Fortunately I have too many important things to cry for . . ."

"No, Don Q, don't you be so outrageous. 'And you will know how to laugh, my son, in order to save the human being's dignity.' Learn to laugh, Don Q."

"Some other day, my dear Josefo, some other day."

On that occasion our conversation ended there.

CHAPTER XXXV: *Wherein the Theme of Laughter, of Baseness, and Other Questions Regarding Existence Are Continued.*

"MY dear Pepe, I was bothered by that business of your laughter," he told me the next time we saw each other. "It was especially disconcerting that you could proclaim that it was something, how did you say it?, that you yourself had gathered in life. Now I understand," he added seriously, "one of the diseases of the will: 'baseness,' which, together with 'abuse' and the roar of thunder make up our people's quaintness."

"Listen, Don Q," I told him, "now you're becoming a bit folkloric and you feel like fighting. What I dared to tell you before was with the best intentions and with the greatest innocence. I think it's one of the things I have gained with time, I believe that . . ."

He didn't let me continue, and interrupted me:

"No, you haven't gained! You have lost. Do you know what that laughter with which you want to fill the ether means? Dignity's laughter, as you called it? It means, Josefo, that you suffer from one of the diseases of the Will: it's called baseness, aggravated in your case because it is a cosmic baseness. Do you know why you let out, better yet, you want to let out those laughs? Because due to your lack of understanding of the order of things in their ultimate circumstances, your sick will of incapacity pretends to relax the universe's austere order, not to save your dignity, a vicious form of Ieity that produces the morbid deviations of your wanting. And you, Josefo, due to your inability to get to the gist of the secret, want to violate it with your laughter, as if, with it, the unknown order would fall to your feet and you would become the world's master, the one who can laugh at the Milky Way. Your laugh is so ridiculous; small in its pretentiousness. Do you realize that I laugh at your laughter?"

Very slowly he let out a forced laugh that was slow and almost rationalized: "Ha! Ha! Ha!"

"Very good, Don Q," I said, "you're learning to Laugh."

"Yes," he continued very seriously, "I let out baseness from your baseness to dialectically restore an order that saddens me to know you have learned to pretend to break with age."

"Listen, Don Q; I don't think things are so bad; nor do I pretend any of that. I simply and innocently laugh, that's all. It's not that much. Don't draw such grave consequences . . . Don't sadden me!"

"You ought to be ashamed, above all because it's a symptom of other grave decadences, which force me to explore more in you. Come on, tell me, besides laughing, what?"

"Don Q man! It's a kind of sudden question. What's what?"

"Don't play stupid! What other novelty have you 'joined' in your life and with age. I refer to, of course, things that you can tell, not the ones you have to hide, which I'm sure you have and which don't interest me. Things that you may tell your children . . ."

"Gosh, Don Q! What do you want me to tell you? Something about my life? What can I tell you that interests you? I have lived, survived, putting my existence in all finite things, absolutely given to transitoriness of time, its pace having been accepted, getting into its everyday matters. What can I tell you that wouldn't be anecdotal? Nothing important to your style. Don't set me on fire. I'm not a prophet or social reformer. I'm not an artist or a guerrilla. I don't explode to bring news to the infinite's corner. Basically nothing, Don Q. A simple and comfortable life in which I have looked for and accepted the fundamental faculties. Nothing heroic. I have compromised. I have fallen to temptation. I have closed certain roads and that's what may interest you. I have closed many roads that I never took, nor will I take: some small, others important . . . each road a great or insignificant decision. It may be the only thing I can tell you: I have made decisions and I am where I am. Nothing important, Don Q! Nothing that may satisfy you, I believe! I have lived every day. I have existed. I have lived existence. Among many roads, I have had the opportunity of taking one and I am on it. Excuse me."

CHAPTER XXXVI: *Wherein, Upon Remembering Wagner, the Road Not Taken Is Considered.*

"WHAT a simple thing! That reminds me of when I was in the other hemisphere. I was rowing in a beautiful lake made of the most beautiful colors and transparencies. Pines, pines all over. A soft fog related everything to a tone from Wagner's music. Everything blue, gray, and green, a bit of purple. Just like Wagner! I recall that on a small embankment, a wide road that ascended and lost itself among the pines, either ended or began. I stopped rowing and I looked at it for a long while. I thought about going to the road and taking it. I thought about the perspective I would have from there; the consistency of the soil, at first muddy near the lake; afterwards loose earth upholstered with pine cones. I imagined the fragrance. Finally, a road, with its sense and details. A road that finally I didn't take. A road that remained there; that I didn't walk on and that I will not see. It remained there with its details and its surprises. There remained a destiny whose possibility I did not confront, because when I stopped rowing, insensibly, the current was taking me towards the rapids and I had to row vigorously to resist the pull going sideways, without going forward or backwards, until I got to the shore and I forgot the road I didn't take, and that I now remember. Then I became aware, my modest Josefo, that human life is only a tape that ends at the tip of a single road, that penetrates the mystery step by step, and that, close to the tip, sets up, at any moment, an infinite and constant current of possibilities from which you have only one opportunity to decide in each moment and in your own space. I do lament that you haven't been consumed; but what can be done? Perhaps, if I had another opportunity, I would travel toward that road and then, perhaps, you by yourself and I on my own, we would consume ourselves. The problem is, I think, to know if we ourselves will be given another possibility of choosing at every moment. Sometimes I think of another madness, which I dare to tell you due to the modesty with which you exist. I think (how can I tell you?) that all consciences will be interchanged and in such a way each conscience will have the opportunity to be in each point of view and enjoy or suffer the interminable chain of possibilities. Do you understand? Judging by your abashed face, you don't understand me. What I mean to say is that you, with your own conscience, are going to brighten other points of view and in such a way that you will be a beggar, king, or jester and you will suffer and commit injustices. You will interchange yourself. Well, I realize this is nothing more than idiocy. I won't go on with this theme. I was only trying to justify your existence, that modest conjunction into which you have sewn yourself to be where you are. And how tranquilly you say to me, 'Don't explode, bring news to the corners of the infinite.' What a shame! Laugh, little Pepe! Laugh that you didn't explode! Laugh!"

And that conversation left me with a vague feeling of sadness, and on that occasion it was I who retired. I confess I would have liked to have given him another . . .

CHAPTER XXXVII: *Wherein Ug's Time in Jail Is Contemplated and Considerations of the World of Paper and Ink Are Formulated, and Wherein Some Reflections on Pain, Copal Gum, and Universal Equilibrium Are Exaggerated.*

"YOU know," Don Q told me on another occasion, "what impressed me when I visited the great Ug in jail? We are living an epoch of constant human pain on paper and ink. That's how future generations will know it: the age of constancies on paper and ink. By means of a paper signed in ink by a man, some people came one day to take Ug to jail and they kept him there I don't know how long. He was, of course, accused of having stolen a valuable coin collection. What the papers said transcended reality, and through a chain of circumstances, very formally expressed on paper, good old Ug found himself enclosed by walls and without liberty. What moved me most is that Ug accepted the situation calmly, and that he never exposed Lu. He withstood the punishment and dishonor.

" 'Like that,' he told me, 'I will be in peace with my conscience.'

He lived for a while with other human beings who were also locked up to atone for their faults. I don't know if the others accepted confinement as Ug did. He was there until an inked paper arrived stating that he could go out because some legal criteria had been satisfied (in which I somehow participated, I must say, so you don't believe that I was indifferent to the plight of that just man). And just as the great Ug had signed in to go to jail, stating that he had done it, he signed upon leaving, stating that he was no longer inside and had regained his freedom.

"The memory of modern humanity is basically made up of paper and ink. Big and small things contained in papers. What a great mass of papers the history of humanity is! How many lost freedoms are written on those papers!

"What's odd is that Ug accepted life behind the walls of the penitentiary as a way of tranquilizing his conscience. A fault I didn't understand because I knew that he had been the simple agent of Lu's decision. Nevertheless, Ug insisted that he had done it, that he had done it willfully, and he answered meekly, admitting he had exchanged his given will for his lost freedom. How odd, don't you think so, Mr. Lawyer? But why am I asking you? Lawyers specialize in that, in exchanging faults for liberty. Honestly, Mr. Lawyer, between you and me, doesn't it seem absurd to you to exchange intentions for liberty?"

"Don Q, sir," I tried to answer, "the social danger manifested by a delinquent when he infringes a mandate typified by society as a crime, sanctionable by imprisonment, evidently has . . ."

"Heavens!" Don Q interrupted me. "You're not in court! Think and you will find it incredibly primitive that society holds that a man will be in peace with society if he spends 'five to eight years' in a 'correctional institution.' See it's penitence again, punishment again! Again someone else's or your own pain, when it's accepted, as Ug did, to pay for things. I must repeat that it's something that obsesses me: pain must really be strange, in the case of pain not being free, of not being able to move, of living abnormally, when society considers itself paid by punishing individuals. Exquisite and valuable coin able to pay what's impossible to acquire: the good or bad past, lost in a time gone by. As far as that—I ask myself—does society resemble the universe, does it have its own chambers of compensation in which pains are tabulated? Are we so made in the image of gods that pain intoxicates us, like incense and copal, to establish that harmony has been restored because an individual has suffered?"

I confess I had never asked myself that question from that point of view, and, as it reached the depths of my professional character, I tried to answer something and said:

"Look, Don Q, it's not precisely pain that society looks for, it simply alienates a rotten apple that . . ."

"Jesus Christ!" Don Q interrupted me again, "what unbearable vulgarity! What a botanical professional deformation! No, my dear lawyer, honor and pride of our forum. A thousand times no! Be serious and sincere. Admit that it's a social acceptance of the law of pain as a redeemer of guilt. It's sacrifice, not on the altar of the gods, but in the majesty of justice. Every day and all over, humanity continues sacrificing, throwing heaps of human pain on the altars of the gods. Notice I don't criticize because, I confess, I find nothing to substitute. I only ask, I ask you as a man of law, you who attend the august tribunals of punishment, is pain the greatest good by dint of being the worse evil? It's evident that the universal consensus of all epochs, from all over, from time immemorial, to our days, has been to consider pain, punishment, sacrifice, guilt, and penitence as payments. Granted that you can exchange the evil you have committed for the pain you suffer. I ask you, Josefo, can you also acquire goods by giving your pain in exchange?

"Now the Indian world or the world of penitents from all over will not seem absurd to you. The serious, lay, organized, electronic, atomic societies of our time, charge, with pain, the evil done to them by those who infringe their norms. Oh, wonderful, primitive societies! How many human pains are kept in their beautiful boxes, perfectly accountable on well-inked paper!

"You know, Josefo, and I will always repeat it to you whenever I discover it, I think that's the most horrendous secret of the universe: the existence of pain and its priceless price to restore history, individual or collective. Pain as an instrument of equilibrium and harmony. Pain will have to be deified. Don't you think so? 'Saint Pain, Martyr, Patron of those who suffer.' What do you think? 'Saint Punishment the Archangel, Patron of Penitentiaries.' 'Saint Torture, Comforting Virgin of All Wars.'

"I'm not so misguided. Look at poor Ug, jailed, with his scraggly black beard grown in captivity, and his resigned look of a chained dog. He paid his debt to society and was freed. In a folder which is probably in some file cabinet, there's proof that he paid his debt, with the punishment 'he served a jail term of . . . ,' his file states. I saw him. I saw him come and go. Of course, I also became aware that he suffered. But precisely because he suffered, a judge, very seriously, representing society, considered that Ug was at peace with his conscience. Everyone is happy!

"Is it not to be considered? Everyone happy, even the one who suffered, because a human being suffered.

"It was also odd to see how good old Ug admitted his situation whenever I rebelled and told him that I thought it unjust and undue that he suffer captivity. I remember that he very conscientiously used to tell me:

" 'Come on, Don Q, don't be afraid! Suffering is a manly thing. That's how they temper themselves and become men. What kind of a man would I be if I were to cry because I'm suffering? Forget about so much running around and let me become a man. I am at the age of suffering and learning! As if pain were something from another world! It's the most natural thing, Q!' Just a bit more and he would have said to me, 'Don't be obstreperous.' I confess to you that I felt a bit ridiculous, like an old woman crying.

"But that doesn't erase the question. Many times I ask myself if just as one considers, even for the imperfect human society, that pain vindicates, is justice done somewhere to those who suffer without guilt? Or to those who suffer because they have no other coin besides their own pain with which to buy? What's going to be given in exchange to restore harmony? I ask you again . . .

"Do you have an answer, my dear Josefo? Have you ever formulated an answer in your life?"

"Come on! What answer can I have? Nothing, my dear Don Q. What the hell do I know about those things that have you so obsessed? Yes, I must tell you that I'm very sorry that Ug had to vindicate his crime."

"But notice that he considered it a good deed. He knew how to make himself his own judge and he didn't forgive himself. He punished himself, by accepting the sentence, until he was at peace with his conscience. Notice how the question reproduces itself at the individual level. He left there feeling better. Feeling more manly! 'Pain is a manly thing,' he told me. The odd thing is that whenever I asked him about Don Lu and I made his conduct seem ugly, good old Ug used to say, 'Don't judge him. He must have reasons that I, in my stupidity, don't understand. He's my friend and that's enough.'

" 'But,' I insisted, 'how is it possible that you not only find it just, but normal, to pay penalties and that you don't want anything for him?'

" 'I'm not nor could I be a judge. To be a judge one must

be wise. One has to know things, and I know little about Lu. I know that he is my friend and that friends love and help each other without thinking about it.'

"Notice, Josefo, how strange: a guy who didn't forgive himself, who was not satisfied with simple repentance; who accepted the punishment. He knew how to forgive. I'm saying it wrong, he didn't even know how to put the blame on someone. How is it possible to only know how to blame oneself? Perhaps, I think, with Ug's example, the only solution may be to be one's own judge. A judge of justice, not of forgiveness, which would then be pulling one's own leg. Don't you think? But there always remains the disquieting reflection that, in every case, some sort of suffering cleanses faults. Why? I ask myself. I can't find the answer. Undoubtedly because of that I ask the same thing so often and then I find another answer, obviously somehow associated with Ug."

CHAPTER XXXVIII: *Wherein St. John of the Cross Is Remembered with All Due Respect.*

" 'IT moves me to see you hanging from a cross and being ridiculed . . .'

"Notice, Josefo, pain as a disinterested love motive and as inspiration for behavior. Wherever I turn my head, wherever I ask my questions, there's always pain or the infinite. That's what has me crushed and because of that I'm never at rest. If you are an individual, you are not infinite. But you then have the aptitude to suffer."

"Come on, Don Q! Again the same theme. What an obsession for pain! I told you already that there's also laughter. Laugh, Don Q!"

"Would you dare to laugh at pain? Someone else's pain? Because you can do whatever you want with yours, you can buy laughter with it if you want. But someone else's pain, a child's pain for example? Would you laugh? Only the devil would laugh at a child's pain. Oh, you, the great master of laughter, the one whose loud laugh fills the voids of ether. Would you be able to laugh at a child's pain?"

"Come on, Don Q! Don't even ask me that. The question alone horrifies me. Only the devil would be able to laugh at a child's pain. There you have it, Don Q, your Lucifer, your admired Lucifer. Can you imagine him laughing at the pains of a child?"

"How terrible it would be for Lucifer's creator that such would be his protest, that he would laugh at pain in such a way!"

"Shut up, Don Q! You really have odd thoughts!"

"Well, don't provoke me, Josefo, you already know that I like to get to the bottom of things. Such is the consequence and the problem of our living in a world created by the two halves, the ones which are in Omeyocan, in Place Two.

"And there's that other answer:

> *'Lord, the heaven you have promised me,*
> *doesn't move me to love you . . .'*

"Neither does hell. Neither reward nor punishment, Mr. Lawyer. Neither reward nor punishment: what moves loving is pain and ridicule. Love admitted precisely to cause love, and love motivated precisely in the admitted love. It's another answer. Don't you think? Did I tell you that some day I would like to cry for him in the Agora? Yes, I already told you, and you let me know that you had already done so.

Pure conduct. Affirmed despite doubt. I believe that deep inside there's a beautiful and solid faith in creation, right? But look at this other attitude: to love and to behave because someone suffered so that I might love and behave. What wonderful humility, to accept someone else's sacrifice! I think it's easy to be the saving hero. A beautiful role. What humility to accept being saved! Note well, Josefo: to accept someone else's pain. In your goodness you dispose of someone else's pain. To accept another's sacrifice. Don't you find it incredibly difficult? That St. John of the Cross is evidently the most humble saint. Do you understand it like that? A will that accepts someone else's sacrifice, that explains and justifies. I believe there's merit on both sides. An authentic communion in pain. A reverse Judas. Do you understand me? There had to be a traitor. How difficult to be it! How much resignation, how much humility, or how much pride to admit it! There have to be some who are saved, redeemed. How much humility to recognize it! Your pain moves me!"

CHAPTER XXXIX: *Final Reflections on Feather Ornaments, Navels, Tunics, and Robes. "I Hope So, Don Q!"*

"LISTEN, Don Q, you really go around things! You are not at rest . . ."

"No, Josefo. I repeat: wherever I turn my head, I find an enigma and many answers. Which is right? I get into all of them. They all disturb me. What a painful condition I have that I can't even doubt! Feather ornaments, navels, tunics, and robes! How can I rest if all of that falls on top of me and dazzles me?"

"Don't worry about me, talking is an outlet, even if it is only with a man like you, so much involved with everyday life, without questions. Don't worry. It's in me to look for answers to my inexhaustible eagerness to pose questions. I'm thinking whether that's the answer, 'your pain moves me.' Did the Indian gods feel like that in front of the offered pain? Is it not a different world, radically different, this one that dealt in our blood? Note well and try to understand: there's someone who, with all humility, upon accepting the gratuitous tribute of pain, converts it to love and goodness. An entire moral world is born, or kept, and it's the same thing. Again the same question, the same disturbing question as soon as you twist the answers a bit: pain to save or create or keep a world. This is the moral world of good behavior. That is the world of suns and jaguars. In the end, order, banishment of chaos, salvation from a world of no risk. How close! How tremendously far! Always pain, suffering, blood, 'that so singular a liquor' of old Faust, also redeemed by the painful love of a woman. 'Time alone, another stroke, its individual impetus held by a rose.' How do you suppose that I'm going to be still if answers are twisted everywhere? I must tire you, I'm sure. It must be tiresome to be hearing this constant reiteration. But think, Mr. Lawyer, it's important things that are repeated to mark universal rhythms. The occasional can or cannot be beautiful, but it's difficult for it to be important: the sun comes up every day and your heart always beats, as long as it is beating. Whatever is important is repeated. Don't be annoyed, then, that I repeat to you what is important."

"Come on, Don Q, it doesn't bother me. Why should it?

I'm aware of the things that bother and obsess you; that, on the other hand, are the things that sometime, somehow, we all ask with some kind of precision. You do it with passion. You do it, I would dare say, with rhythm."

"But what's the answer?"

"Probably all of them, Don Q, as long as they are authentic and sincere."

"That's precisely where my problem lies, Don Pepe. I understand them all, I explain them all. What's more: I accept them all, but I definitely don't behave like any of them. I embrace them all, I fondle them, but to none do I give myself with the explosive passion of prototypes. And that's another one of my anxieties, Josefo: you understand that my life is not a problem of intelligence but rather of will, it's resolving myself to be, or better yet, to become something and not to dilute myself in everything. That's another one of my problems: to understand too much and not to give up my radical will to anything. To have my will attached to my intelligence. I understand perfectly, dear Josefo Guillermo, why don't you set yourself on fire! Why you didn't explode! You were lacking the definitive will that I also lack. I am only a source, seemingly unending, of words, comprehensions, reasons, wrongs, and paradoxes. And how do I behave? Have I given a pain for something? Have I separated myself to renounce my Ieity? Have I accepted someone else's pain to redeem myself? Have I even rebelled? Not at all! Words, words, words. Logos, verb and literature. That: pure Logos, Verb and Literature. And my will? To whom or why have I given it? Pure dilution of understanding. Pure reasoning, denial, and, on certain occasions, self-resignation. And my will, Josefo? To what have I given my will? I criticize you because you didn't explode! I'm sad, Josefo, with my weak will attached to my understanding. What have I done! There's the question. What have you done, Josefo, what have you done? With your will to do, to behave, to create, what have you done?"

"Nothing important, Don Q. And you?"

"Nothing important, Don Pepe.

"You know, Pepe, to reflect things is to understand them. It's to have the windows open so that light comes in. It's conscience. To do them is another thing, it's to participate in creation. A tip of an infinite tape, it's true. But one thing is to go on like a little mirror and another to go on like a drill. Hopefully your will will not become sick or withered. I believe that's where the best in humanity lies: in the will and not in representation. I haven't even, like the good Ug, constructed my mind's peace by accepting a punishment or a reparation.

"Perhaps some day I or you, Josefo, will find something for which to give up your will."

"I hope so, Don Q!"

The Spaniard didn't brutally conquer mexico.
They didn't kill the indians like the anglo-saxons did and we mexicans are proof of that with our spanish and indian blood.
Lopez Portillo may sound all the mexican he wants to.
But the fact is that he is a Jew if not by convictions at least by race. Just like Columbus was and so many distinguish man in history